WANDERER

WANDERER

SARAH LÉON

Translated from the French by John Cullen

OTHER PRESS / NEW YORK

Copyright © Éditions Héloïse d'Ormesson 2016
Originally published in French as *Wanderer* in 2016
by Éditions Héloïse d'Ormesson, Paris
English translation copyright © Other Press 2019

Production editor: Yvonne E. Cárdenas
Text designer: Jennifer Daddio / Bookmark Design & Media
This book was set in Horley Old Style by
Alpha Design & Composition of Pittsfield, NH

1 3 5 7 9 10 8 6 4 2

LIBRARY OF CONGRESS CATALOGING-IN-PUBLICATION DATA

Names: Léon, Sarah, 1995- author. | Cullen, John, 1942- translator.
Title: Wanderer / Sarah Léon ; translated from the French by John Cullen.
Other titles: Wanderer. English
Description: New York : Other Press, 2018.
Identifiers: LCCN 2018013941 (print) | LCCN 2018017170 (ebook) |
ISBN 9781590519264 (ebook) | ISBN 9781590519257 (pbk.)
Subjects: LCSH: Piano teachers—Fiction. | Pianists—Fiction. |
Teacher-student relationships—Fiction.
Classification: LCC PQ2712.E65 (ebook) | LCC PQ2712.E65 W3613 2018 (print) |
DDC 843/.92—dc23
LC record available at https://lccn.loc.gov/2018013941

Sie liebten sich beide, doch keiner
Wollt' es dem anderen gesteh'n—
Sie sahen sich an so feindlich,
Und wollten vor Liebe vergeh'n.

■

They loved each other, but neither
Would venture to speak thereof;
They glared at each other like enemies
And wanted to die of love.

HEINRICH HEINE

He goes. Through woods, across fallow fields, over sleeping, frost-covered hills. A wandering silhouette, lost in the surrounding whiteness, sinking deeper and deeper into the peaty hollows, down to the heart of the crusted ice.

For some time now, he's been softly chanting—rather than singing—the words of a beloved lied.

Ich wandle still, bin wenig froh,
und immer fragt der Seufzer, wo?*

He lingers over those first three words, "Ich wandle still"; never have they sounded more fitting than in this place, at this moment, murmured by a solitary man. They are the Logos of

---

* "Silent I wander, my joys are rare, / And every sigh is a question: where?" (from *"Der Wanderer"* [The Wanderer]).

1

the beginning, thus intoned in a universe returned to its starting point by the grace of cold and savage winter, "der Winter kalt und wild."

He traverses shady woodlands, where shafts of sudden light dazzle him; he crosses frozen streams and walks along the edge of a pond whose violet waters are shot through with iridescence; chunks of ice bob in the pond with a sound like rustling silk. Farther on, a Wasserfall* splashes him. Wisps of mist seem to be suspended above the ground, sometimes clinging to a treetop or a blasted trunk.

He rediscovers the beauty of winter. He loves it.

Suddenly he stops and leans against a stump. He's turned pale. A stone cross disfigured by lichen is standing at a crossroads. He contemplates the cross for a moment. He goes on his way.

---

* Waterfall.

1

ON THE ICY RIVER

The Pommier Chenin (originally the name of a kind of apple tree) was a structure, for all intents and purposes in ruins, that Hermin had managed to render habitable despite the inhospitality of the lower foothills of the Bourbonnais. The squat building's stone façade had been standing up to heavy rains and icy blasts for at least two centuries, proving by that very fact how staunchly it could resist the interminable winters. Nevertheless, its isolation, more than anything else, left it exposed to the cold of the dark months, and the young composer often found himself cut off from the nearest village by a virtually impassable accumulation of snow. At such times he had to stay shut up for days in what he ironically called "the Great Room" until he felt he could safely venture outside. Needless to say, during those periods he had very few visitors. Who would have dared defy the elements to reach him?

And yet, on a January evening when darkness was falling, there was one who dared. The only one imaginable, the master of the dazzling gesture, the friend who had one day vanished: Lenny.

"*Ich bin wiedergekommen,*" was all the apparition from the past said, but with a smile.

Hermin froze. Ten years of absence, ten years without music, without words—and now, to reconnect, one simple sentence: *I'm back.* That was the boy, all right…

To come to where Hermin was, Lenny must have traveled so many snowy miles, so many muddy paths! Lenny's passion for long hikes and the nickname he'd been given were of course well known to Hermin; but Lenny's rambles, in his memory, had remained more literary than real, and he was surprised to see that the young man had chosen—in the middle of January—to swap his copy of Liszt's *Années de pèlerinage* for hiking boots. And besides, to disappear in the heart of the Monts de la Madeleine, to abandon rehearsals and concerts to pay him a visit, him, after ten years of oblivion! Hermin was stunned. What common ground could there be at this point between the composer holed up in the depths of the forest and the young pianist with the entire musical world at his feet? Love for Schubert, no doubt; but what else?

"You decided it was time for your *Winter Journey*, is that it?" Hermin asked jokingly.

Lenny smiled another small smile and said, "In a way..."

His silhouette stood out against the background of the snow-covered slope. Although his features were drawn by fatigue, his eyes shone. Almost laughing, he added, "Admit it, you were not expecting this."

Which was putting it mildly. A teenager had left him; a man had returned.

"Well, you *have* taken me by surprise," said Hermin, who was nevertheless quite aware that the boy had always been surprise incarnate, that the role he played was the unexpected guest, the stranger passing through: on this evening, he came as a vagabond seeking shelter for a night, and that was all.

As his only reply, Lenny shrugged his shoulders. Then, casting a quick glance around, he said, "I never thought you would leave your garret for burying yourself here..."

"Solitude is composition's surest ally."

This was as good a reply as any; Hermin wasn't certain he believed it. "You must be tired," he went on, pulling his friend into the Great Room, which would have seemed quite shabby had the fire not enriched it with sooty and golden-brown reflections that danced in the darkness on the furniture huddled around the hearth. Instead of switching on the lamp, Hermin grabbed two bronze candlesticks to prolong the spell. A light gleamed in the boy's eyes.

"I remember I got those from a junk dealer!"

"As you see, I still have them."

Dust from the pianos danced in the sunbeam filtering in through the shop's half-open door...

Hermin disappeared. He returned a moment later with a savory pie and two plates, which he put down without saying a word. Equally mute, Lenny watched him; it seemed that each of their movements complied with a liturgy whose proceedings must at all costs remain uninterrupted. Outside, the darkening sky added to the fragility of the instant. It was raining melted snow.

It took a long time for the conversation to get under way. Where to begin after such a long silence? Hermin, agitated, was looking for some suitable words to say, words neither too laden with meaning nor too trivial—words, in short, that might revive the best of their friendship while steering clear of quarrels, misunderstandings, and remorse.

"Tell me about these past years," he said at last. "At first, I thought you'd get lost in Paris for a few weeks and then cry for help. Apparently I didn't know you very well..."

"That is what I did the first few days, I was lost in the streets. Then I got a piano job in a bar... I almost ruined my technique, pounding an old clunker every night! I missed the Zimmermann, you know—"

"Well, take a look, there it is!"

Lenny turned toward the instrument Hermin was pointing at. His face lit up, and he made a move in the direction of what had been his first piano. His young composer friend could never make up his mind to abandon it, even though these days he hardly made use of it anymore. But the piano's history seemed so closely connected to theirs...

Dust from the pianos danced in the sunbeam filtering in through the shop's half-open door. I was settled in a corner, studying my harmony course. To fund my studies, I'd taken a job as a salesman for a piano maker. Customers were rare...

"Anyway, some people noticed me, they got me a scholarship, a professor took me under his wing, then he arranged some recitals, like you the first—"

One fall morning he entered the shop and slowly moved through it, fascinated by the instruments: a Pleyel concert grand, a Gaveau beginners' upright, completely inlaid, some lacquered Steinways...

"You already knew enough to make a career when you left me!"

I went up to him. He was young—fifteen or so—and he hadn't come to buy anything, but he asked permission to try the instruments. His awkward syntax and German accent added to his shyness. A bit puzzled, I gave my consent. He sat on one of the benches, positioned his hands on the piano, and

touched the keys in a way both respectful and resolute. Then
he started to play.

At that time of evening, the collapsing flames gave the
room the look of a ship in disarray; Hermin, standing at the
rail, could never get over the sight. Arabesques of mingled
ash and gold passed before his eyes while the wind mounted
a fierce attack on the Pommier Chenin.

It wasn't what I'd expected, one of those "repertory
pieces" that beginning students bang out gracelessly, unable
to distinguish the prelude from the fugue, the theme from its
variations. Nor was it jazz, in spite of certain rhythms. It was
an improvisation. At first hesitant, his playing grew more and
more confident, almost audacious; he played tense chords,
essayed various improbable progressions, and suspended some
cadences, evidently indifferent to the laws of harmony. Most
of all, he listened to himself, strangely marveling; his fin-
gers seemed to be discovering the piano, wandering back and
forth over the keyboard, delicate, nimble, and nevertheless
powerful—but it was as if they were doing so for the first time.
A vague uneasiness came over me.

"Time sure has passed quickly," Hermin murmured,
detaching—not without an effort—his eyes from the
fireplace.

"How old are you?"

"Thirty-three."

"The age of Christ…"

"Can I be entering the time of the Passion?"

They exchanged an almost knowing look. Hermin turned away to pour two glasses of new wine. Silence fell again, broken only by gusts of wind. An unspoken question was floating between them, separating them like a curtain.

"*Den Tag des ersten Grusses, / Den Tag, an dem ich ging; / Um Nam' und Zahlen windet / Sich ein zerbroch'ner Ring*," Lenny murmured by way of response.

"Translation?" the young composer joked, certain that he'd recognized some verses from Schubert's song *"Auf dem Flusse,"* one of the lieder in his *Winterreise*, the "Winter Journey" they'd listened to more fervently than to any other song cycle...

"'The day of our first meeting, the day I went away; and around the name and dates, a broken ring.'"

"A broken ring," Hermin echoed him.

How long did he play that day? Most likely not so long as he does in my memory, but wonderment had more or less suspended time for me. He stopped playing without concluding, stood up, and prepared to leave the shop...

"But tell me," Lenny went on, preferring to change the subject, "what did you do after I left?"

"Nothing...not much..." Hermin answered sincerely.

The fabric of his life had slowly worn itself out during those years of virtual solitude. After the *allegro vivace* that had marked the rhythm of their two years together—*so rasch wie möglich*, in his friend's language, "as fast as possible"—he'd settled into an irresolute *moderato* before leaving the city and taking refuge in the solitude of the Pommier Chenin. Could that exile have made any sense other than as an attempt to embalm the memory of the young man, to freeze time until the improbable moment of his return?

I put a hand on his shoulder to hold him back. "Are you taking piano lessons?"

He shook his head. Now he seemed hurried, restless, as if he regretted his boldness. "Ich kann nicht…*I do not really know how to play…I must to go now…"*

"You…listen, on this subject, I think I know what I'm talking about: if you're not a pianist yet, you'll soon become one!"

"I must to go," the boy repeated in a muffled voice.

Once again, silence fell on them, imposing itself like an unwanted guest. Each of their words seemed to remain implicit; it wasn't a matter of incomprehension—not yet—but the rift hollowed out by absence was proving hard to fill.

The young composer observed Lenny surreptitiously. He hardly ate anything, he who had always been famished as a teenager; it was as if a sort of reticence kept him aloof from his plate and his cutlery, but he drank a lot. A strange flame had begun to glow in his very black eyes, as if he were drunk—but perhaps his distraction wasn't due to alcohol alone. The candlelight threw tawny reflections on his face, which he seemed to be practically offering to his older friend's furtive contemplation. On the whole, Hermin thought as he looked at him, Lenny had barely changed; he was as handsome as ever, in spite of his pallor, his sharp cheekbones, in spite of the years that had passed. Some of his black locks had strayed onto his forehead, but it didn't occur to him to push them back. He wasn't smiling; his smiles had always been rare. The young composer had often pondered what might lie behind his friend's habitual silence; this evening, more than ever, Hermin was utterly in the dark as to Lenny's thoughts or the adversities he might have suffered. As far as Hermin was concerned, Lenny had just well and properly completed his Winter Journey. He imagined him hiking through forests and villages, like the rambler in the beloved lieder cycle, sometimes accompanied by a crow that showed him the way, sometimes spotting a weather vane as fickle as his mood, or maybe coming upon a lime tree, the lovely tree of memory; walking beside a river full of ice floes, barked at by village dogs, refused a room at the inn; then waking at dawn on a stormy morning; and finally meeting the organ grinder from the previous day: "Strange old man, shall I come with you?..."

The youth sat up straight, stretched a little, and emptied his wineglass, as though hastening the end of the meal;

then Hermin, who had just come out of his daydream, asked him a question, his voice hurried, doubtless for fear of the response he was going to get: in memory of their evenings long ago, would Lenny play something?

Ordinarily, you don't invite a concert pianist, out of the blue, to exhibit his talent; that sort of proposition is reserved for children whose parents, bursting with pride, want their offspring's ability—or what they consider as such—to be admired. Hermin was not unaware of this, and he was troubled by the idea that Lenny could take offense at being still regarded as the student, the protégé—in short, *the kid*. Yet his reaction bore a curious resemblance to that image: he bit his lip, like a child whose disobedience has just been brought to light, and he replied in a voice that suddenly sounded hesitant: "There is something I have not told you yet."

It took him a moment to find the words, and then he went on, feeling his older friend's eyes fixed on him: "I have...canceled all my concerts."

Feigning composure, Hermin picked up his glass.

One thing was certain: the boy was already a pianist— from all eternity and forever.

"You mean...you're calling off the whole season?"

The young man shook his head. "No. I mean I am giving up the profession."

And just as Hermin had thought he'd understood, when he heard his friend play for the first time, that he was a pianist *from all eternity and forever,* in that later moment he understood that Lenny's decision was irrevocable; never again, he could be certain of it, would he hear the song of the boy whom those who knew him had nicknamed—because he too had soles of wind, and because he played Schubert's music better than anyone else—"the Wanderer."

2

FROZEN TEARS

The first days passed in silence and intense cold. No stove, no fireplace was able to relieve the dampness in the dwelling or heat it sufficiently. The young composer never saw winter coming without a touch of uneasiness, and he regretted the fact that Lenny, fragile as he was, had chosen precisely the first days of the year to come and join him. The young man, however, had made no complaint and even had to be urged to accept the loan of some of Hermin's woolen clothing. Lenny had arrived at the Pommier Chenin nearly empty-handed, as if he had desired to abandon, at the same time as his pianistic career, the few relics every man takes on over the course of years. He had provided no account of the reasons that had led him to come and find his friend in his retreat and settle in there himself, nor any explanations relating to his decade-long absence. Hermin hadn't ventured to question him.

Besides, they didn't talk much. The first evening hadn't sufficed to animate their silences or curtail their hesitations; and it didn't seem that the passing days had achieved any greater success in reestablishing their former bond. Hermin had indeed tried to question the young man about the reasons for his choice, his desire to give up the piano, a step that Hermin considered a mere whim, but he had come up against evasive words that contained no genuine response. He'd abandoned his career, and everything had lapsed into silence.

Over the next several weeks, I saw no more of the boy who had burst into the store like a shooting star and then left without a word of farewell. Perhaps, with time, I would have forgotten about him; but things didn't go like that. It was written that our paths would cross again.

Hermin saw little of his guest during the day; Lenny joined him only at breakfast and then again at supper, after which they generally passed the evening in the Great Room, exchanging a few words from time to time. The young composer didn't know how Lenny spent his days, holed up in the little room he'd moved into. Freed from the routine of arduous daily practice on his instrument, Lenny didn't seem very eager to engage in any other activity. As a boy, he'd been a reader; he used to recite Rimbaud in German:

*"Ich schrieb das Schweigen, die Nächte…Ich hielt den Taumel fest."** These performances would amuse Hermin. At the moment, though, he was worried about the idleness that seemed to have seized hold of his friend, but he didn't dare say anything.

One evening I went to the Conservatory, intending to find a room to practice in—my rented garret's neighbors having expressed their irritation at constantly hearing me through walls and partitions—and opened the door of a studio I knew would be unoccupied at that hour…

When he wasn't in his room or sunk in an armchair before the fire, the young man prowled the house, small though it was, from cellar to attic; he apparently enjoyed going up and down the staircase with the questionable steps or pacing the worn tiles in the hall on the upper floor, adding his own invisible footprints to those of so many generations. In a word, he roamed. Maybe he was only trying to keep warm. From time to time, he gave a little cough, but Hermin could never determine whether it was due to the dampness or to nervousness.

He was there, seated at the piano with his hands on the keyboard. I saw him turn pale and get up from his bench.

"I thought you told me you weren't a Conservatory student," I said, a little disappointed.

---

* *"J'écrivais des silences, des nuits…Je fixais des vertiges."* (From *Une saison en enfer*: "I wrote down silences and nights…I held vertigo fast.")

16

"But it is the truth! No one must know I am here!"

To have found Lenny again just as he was abandoning his art: that was what the young composer couldn't bring himself to accept. Music had always governed their friendship; it was from music that their relationship had sprung— from music, and most of all *in* music. To forfeit music was tantamount to letting silence fall between them. Could it be, therefore, that their former harmonies, which once filled the private space of Hermin's garret room, had masked the poverty of their daily exchanges, and that their friendship had been nothing but a simple matter of convenience? And yet Hermin could still remember aimless conversations, exhilarating moments whose connection to music was extremely vague or, more accurately, nonexistent. So what? Rimbaud may well have, as he said, missed the Europe of "the age-old parapets," but what Hermin missed was the music *aux anciens parapets.*

More than anything else, he missed the depth of Lenny's playing, a depth that was equaled only by the pianist's casual manner. In fact, even in those days, the young man's discreet virtuosity and bright, crisp style were already at the service of a rare understanding of the works he interpreted. The semidarkness that Lenny required onstage during his concerts no doubt contributed to the impression they made, but there was more to it than that. Cracks opened up here and there in the music, fissures in a too-perfect edifice, and they gave his art the unsettled, crepuscular color that was his alone. The unique character of his interpretations—particularly those of Schubert's last sonatas, which had gained him the admiration of an audience of refined music lovers—was the work of an artist of chiaroscuro, of light and shade, out of which a luminous line of melody would abruptly emerge. His was an art on the verge of the abyss. Which doubtless explained his fame.

But there was more. Unknown countries seemed to rise up from under his fingertips. As for Hermin, he would think about Schumann's "*fremden Länder,*" those strange landscapes that likewise suited Lenny's singular way of being in the world. So his wild playing, for those who listened to it attentively, evoked an ineffable nostalgia. And on the day when the young composer finally accepted Lenny's music with all that it might contain of a *course à l'abîme,* a race to the abyss, he had to surrender to the evidence: the name of the boy's genius was Despair.

That was something Hermin might have understood from the beginning; he might have understood the tragic dimension of Lenny's being and the thirst for the absolute against which he would struggle in vain. In this sense, Schubert, whom he had placed at the center of his art, was really his brother, transcending the years. The Austrian composer's continual hesitations, his breaks in rhythm, the phrases he couldn't resolve—they were Lenny's too.

With determination, I closed and bolted the door of the practice room. My decision was taken; I had too much regretted watching him disappear the first time to accept a second, definitive vanishing.

Hermin for his part passed the bulk of his days in a hut built not far from the Pommier Chenin, on the edge of the little wood that overlooked his house; he called this rudimentary shelter his "music pavilion," because it was there that he usually composed. All his scores, all his sketches, and all his recordings were gathered together there; the hut also contained his cello, an instrument he'd studied longer and more assiduously than the piano and to which he'd finally dedicated himself. But the keyboard retained the prestige of representing the first bond established between Lenny and him after "chance" had brought them together, though chance evidently doesn't exist in this world. As Hermin well knew—mostly through music, that sovereign divinity, that inexpressible force to which he'd consecrated himself since childhood, and in which nothing, not absence, not even suffering, would ever be able to shake his faith. Of course, he had passed through occasional periods of doubt and discouragement; composition was a ferocious art— "Many are called, few are chosen," as his writing teacher would intone—and particularly risky in a time when both public and promoters were turning away from so-called contemporary music. "We modern composers, painters

of ruin," concluded his older colleague Gérard Pesson...
And how many times had Hermin been able to count on
the fingers of one hand the number of audience members
attending the premiere performance of one of his pieces!
But he had persevered. When Lenny arrived at the Pommier Chenin, the young composer had just completed a
song cycle on poems by Paul Celan, and he was hesitating to
choose among several new projects. His friend's unexpected
return had given him the impetus to embark on a large-scale
work he'd been thinking about for a long time without ever
taking it on: an *Homage to Schubert* for chamber ensemble,
a piece that would mingle various Schubertian themes in the
form of a collage. Seized by sudden ardor, Hermin had has-
tened to take down from the shelves where they lay sleeping
many of the beloved Franz's scores: trios, quartets, quintets,
fantasias, impromptus, and *moments musicaux*, along with
the three cherished lieder cycles, *Die Schöne Müllerin* (The
Beautiful Milleress), *Winterreise* (Winter Journey), and
Schwanengesang (Swan Song), whose pages still bore the
numerous annotations he'd made for Lenny's benefit. The
two of them had often interpreted those pieces together, with
the boy at the piano and Hermin singing as best he could,
and sometimes reversing the roles, so that Lenny bestowed
on Müller's poems his German diction and his raspy voice!
They'd been happy then... or had they?

"*What are you doing here?*"

"I am trying to work. I am hiding..."

"I have no intention of turning you in."

The boy gave the door a furtive glance. "Do you swear?"

Hermin loved spending long hours in his pavilion, loved it so much that he wouldn't give it up, not even in winter; when he left the house to compose, he was dressed like a lumberjack—heavy shirt, sweater, padded leather vest, fingerless gloves—because the only way to heat the hut was to light a fire in the hearth. His ritual was to play a few virtuoso pieces on his cello by way of warming up, and he'd become so used to working in such conditions that he no longer paid them any attention. Above all, he wished to take advantage of the place as long as it remained reachable, knowing that a storm could cut off his access to the wood from one day to the next. But he hadn't dared to bring Lenny there, despite feeling an urgent certainty that the charms of the music pavilion would revive old memories. He so wanted his younger friend to recollect, as he did, the days they'd shared together...

"I must to go now," he said again.

"Not before you answer some questions: Who are you, where do you come from, why don't you enroll in a piano class?"

His cheeks flushed. "The Conservatory is not for me."

One afternoon, as he was leaving the Pommier Chenin to go to his pavilion, Hermin heard a voice calling him; Lenny was looking down from the window of his room on the second floor. "Are you going out?"

Hermin hesitated for a moment. "I'm going to the pavilion" would have been a sign to the young man that his company wasn't wanted; after a pause, Hermin decided to change his tack: "I'm going for a hike. Want to come with me?"

"Wait for me, I will be right there!"

While his friend was getting ready, Hermin went over to the lean-to to check his supply of firewood. He would have to split some logs soon if he didn't want to run short of burnable wood during snowstorm season. But for the time being, the winter seemed to be offering one of its most beautiful days, pure and icy like crystal embedded in rock. White streaks, gelid droplets—like the *Gefrorne Tränen*, the "frozen tears" in the song from *Winterreise* that Lenny was so fond of—decorated the firs with pearls, and a thin layer of frost covered the paved courtyard, iridescent with reflections. Hermin smiled. He loved the apparent fragility of winter, the branches like appliqués on a cobwebby white background different from the whiteness of snow; he loved the landscape that the layer of cold had not entirely covered, for he found there the combination of toughness and vulnerability that had attached him to Lenny. Tough and vulnerable: that was how he'd appeared to him from the very first day. Ten years later, nothing seemed to have changed…

"Listen," I said to him—spontaneously using the familiar form of the verb as I contemplated his hollow cheeks, his

raggedy clothes, his look of a child grown up too soon—"would you like me to teach you to play, just for the pleasure of it?"

He looked me up and down incredulously. I myself didn't know what had pushed me to make such a proposition. I had friends and a job, I was enrolled in courses, and my pianistic capabilities hardly surpassed those of a third-year student, for my chief areas of interest were the cello and composition...

Lenny, dressed in his black coat, stepped over the threshold of the door. The young composer noticed that he'd taken the trouble to comb his hair.

"Are you ready?"

After a silence, he agreed. I scribbled my address on a scrap of paper and handed it to him. Then I let him leave, doubtful in spite of his assent that I'd be seeing him again all that soon.

Lenny nodded.

"All right, then. Let's go."

3

THE SIGNPOST

They had taken only a few steps before Lenny noticed the sign—hanging askew on its post and eaten away like a piece of flotsam—that indicated the name of the place. He stopped. "I wanted to ask you," he said. "Why 'Pommier Chenin'?"

Hermin smiled and without saying a word led his friend to the little fir copse that overlooked his property. There, sheltered from the wind by a ruined wall, the remains of a former outbuilding, crouched a small, shivering tree, drawing toward itself thin branches half-covered by snow. After a few seconds, Lenny's eyes opened wide. "But…it's still bearing fruit!"

Indeed, some wrinkled little apples like Christmas ornaments were barely visible at the top of the tree. Hermin picked up a dead branch that was lying on the ground and vigorously whacked the trunk. His friend caught an apple in the palm of his hand and gazed at the fruit with a sort of childish pleasure, indifferent to the ice crystals that covered it and to the snow that had fallen on him too.

"I did not think this was possible!" he exclaimed.

"The first snow preserves the apples that haven't fallen yet. And believe me, they're the best ones."

Lenny gave him a pensive look. "*Chenin*, what does that mean?"

"'Sour,' or rather, 'tangy.' It refers to the way the apples taste…"

The boy's smile faded a little. He nodded and kept quiet.

I was mistaken. Not long after our meeting, he knocked on my door, and I gave him his first piano lesson. A few days later, he was back; soon after that, we fell into the habit of weekly lessons, which never occurred at a fixed time. He would tell me neither the day nor the hour, contenting himself with climbing up to my garret, ringing my doorbell, and—if I was out—waiting for me; on the only occasion when I dared to suggest a more regular schedule, his eyes turned hard and he answered, in a tone that admitted no reply, that he could change nothing. This irregularity in our hours no doubt contributed, without my noticing it, to distancing me from my friends at the time, compelled as I was to stay home and wait for a boy who didn't always show up; little by little, Nicolas, Charlotte, Iris, and the others got used to seeing me abandon the *"little circle,"* and our slow separation marked the beginning of a new age.

After a pause, Hermin cleared his throat, preparing to counter Lenny's strange fit of melancholy. "Let's go!" he exclaimed.

"Go where?"

"The closest is Moulin-Gaucher, Gaucher's Mill, or a hamlet called Goutaudier...And then there's the Horse Pond, l'Étang-aux-Chevaux, but the roads probably haven't been cleared yet. Farther away, there's Les Biefs and another hamlet known as Les Allemagnes, the Germanies—"

"The Germanies?" Lenny asked, interrupting him.

His face had brightened at the mention of the name. Hermin smiled in his turn. "It's hardly more than a group of abandoned farm buildings..."

"Not a problem!"

The young composer could have cited the cold, the snow, the onset of night, but he knew that nothing would discourage Lenny. His nostalgia for the country of his birth—his Schubertian *geliebtes Land*—was as integral a part of his way of being in the world as his love for wandering or his race to the abyss. Everything in him denoted the existence of a "pale mother," the lamentation for a Germany devastated and poorly reconstructed. These feelings showed in his dark eyes, which retained the image of another land, and in the bitterness that sometimes pursed his lips. They even showed in his silence. Lenny had left Berlin with his aunt at the age of thirteen; after entering France, they'd gone to Paris and settled there. That was all Hermin knew about Lenny's childhood. Hermin was slightly ashamed to realize that in six years he'd never reflected on the meaning of the hamlet's name, and he limited himself to a gesture indicating its direction.

As a student, Lenny proved disconcerting and hard to control: sometimes timid and docile, sometimes recalcitrant, immovably obstinate, or as some would have described him, intolerable—which was, in fact, the case on the rare occasions when I introduced him to people. But I didn't get discouraged, far from it; I remained stunned by his apparently limitless musical and technical abilities, and with each lesson I marveled a little more at his capacity for learning.

In the beginning, they moved along without speaking, but their silence was still neutral, with no hint of mutual agreement or incomprehension, and above all, no indifference. It was up to them to carry out the alchemical operation which, by means of a few words, would give that silence meaning. In short, their destiny had to be played out there, in a snowy landscape that the wandering stranger of the *Winterreise* could have traversed before them; and what could be more appropriate for a man whose friends called him "the Wanderer"? The layer of slick ice on the road provided an excellent pretext for keeping their eyes on the ground, thus avoiding any real engagement in conversation. Instinctively, the two young men had lowered their heads, sensing the importance the least of their words might assume and less than eager to take on the responsibility of speaking them. Too many unanswered questions, too much muffled resentment hovered in the air between them. To express those things frankly would be to risk a great deal; but to restrict themselves to superficial chatter would confirm the falseness of a situation that had lasted only too long.

Once again, Hermin's mind went back to those *"unwirtbaren Wege,"* the inhospitable paths sung by the Romantics. Today, one of them, as though fallen into this century, was trudging through the snow beside him. Lenny had the handsome profile and the wild gaze of his predecessors, and above all he had the indefinable gift of entering at once into a kind of accord with whatever place he was in, of becoming a "participant" in it, like a silhouette a painter adumbrates in a corner of his picture. Now that he was there again, he seemed never to have stopped being there, so much did his silhouette, his bearing, his blank stare harmonize with the surrounding landscape. The young composer was unsettled by this. A thousand times he had imagined the joy he'd feel if his friend should return to his side; but now the thing seemed so natural that it aroused almost no emotion in him, and he was content to welcome it with a sort of detachment— it was the way things *were*, and that was all.

Once or twice, I also ran into him at the Conservatory. When I asked him why he was there, he told me he had no keyboard and he really needed to practice between lessons; I suggested he could come to the store and play on one of the keyboard instruments in the showroom. He nodded, but he seemed reluctant. Not long afterward, I decided to give him a copy of my house key so that he could practice in the calm of the garret when I wasn't there. That time, he gladly accepted.

However, the silence started to seem interminable, threatening to become more awkward than the words that had to be said, so the young composer resolved to speak. "Well, does this look like Germany?" he asked, using a joking tone.

Lenny took time to reflect on his answer.

"It looks like you."

Hermin gave him a questioning look. Had he himself Hermin—ever ceased to think that the boy was an emanation of the landscape, or rather that the landscape was an emanation of the boy?

"What makes you say that?"

"I do not know...you seem to belong here."

Intrigued, the young composer cast his eyes around him. The countryside displayed its wintry charm, and the snow, in its double role of obstacle and enchantment, seemed to have put itself at his service. It cunningly sought to impede the walker, melting in cold trickles down the back of his neck, causing him to stumble at each step, but at the same time offering him itself, dazzling white or sometimes iridescent with gray or nacreous hues, yet always beautiful and wild, like one of those *Schneefräulein*, those "snow-maidens" who inhabit the Germanic imagination.

"If you say so…"

He puzzled me in many ways. Sometimes he'd arrive at an hour when every fifteen-year-old boy is normally sitting in a classroom, listening to a physics or geography teacher drone on about his subject. There were also times when he'd show up at my place after more than a week's absence, tottering from fatigue, his features pale and drawn. One evening I found him sound asleep on the sofa I used as a bed, and I didn't awaken him, so exhausted did he seem.

"It's strange, because the landscape makes me think of you, not me," Hermin went on, after a pause. "You know, 'the Wanderer'!"

Lenny made a face. "It is the journalists who call me that."

"You don't like it?"

"You are not a journalist."

Silence fell again.

He gradually came to take up more and more space in my life, but I was far from being upset by that. Then I became aware of what was happening and decided not to let it continue; I was starting to miss my old friends.

Now they were walking along an unmarked and therefore uncertain path, whose trace was obscured by a mixture of mud and snow. Without the reference point formed by the bell tower of the neighboring village's church, whose spire stood out against the horizon, it would hardly have been prudent to plunge into the countryside; they had likewise to dread the fog, which could at any moment envelop the land in an opaque cloud, and to fear the underbrush, which masked the valley. Aside from some rugged woodcutters, the brave souls who ventured, in the dead of winter, into this notch in the Montagne Bourbonnaise were rare. The large village nearest the Pommier Chenin was about six miles away; there were smaller ones, hamlets really, nestled deep in the countryside, groups of three or four farmhouses fearfully pressing against one another, many of them abandoned, and all evoking the solitude in which Hermin lived six months out of every year. But the young composer, although he wasn't a native of the region, had fallen in love with it, a land where modernity had not yet made its appearance, without a doubt, he had seen in those dense pine forests, in those impetuous waterfalls, in those mist-shrouded mountaintops, the concrete expression of his own most fundamental inclinations. For it was none other than the powerful spirit of the *Sturm und Drang** movement

---

* Literally "Storm and Drive"; often translated as "Storm and Stress."

that seemed to breathe over the land in the bleak months, reviving a world most dear to his heart. And to tell the whole truth, his fondness for a region where one could find, as if gone astray, a parcel of Germany—even if it was a fantasized Germany, more literary than real—had yet another origin. Lenny had, unbeknownst to him, guided Hermin's choice, first by breathing his "Germanness" into his friend's heart, and then by making him desire, after Lenny's departure, a place where his memory could live on. Indeed, from the very first day when the young composer had arrived to take up residence in the Pommier Chenin, he'd never explored the surrounding area without being accompanied by the boy's wandering shadow—and now here he was, the shadow had taken on form and color, and they were walking side by side.

One day I listened to him play his lesson and then told him that he could stay and work on it some more if he wanted to, but that I had a rendezvous with a girlfriend. His face darkened. The girl's name was Iris.

Hermin again looked surreptitiously at the young man, and in spite of Lenny's recent protest, it seemed to Hermin that no nickname had ever been more appropriate. Under his breath, he recited some lines of verse:

The steps you take
On the heather moor
Dust clouds awake

Whose breath is sour.
Traveler so blue,
*Where to? Where to?**

Lenny stopped walking. "Are you really asking that question?"

"What question?"

"The one about which way I am going."

Caught off guard, Hermin stopped in his turn.

"I don't know. If you intend to answer it, then yes."

But the boy likewise opted for a quotation: *"Eine Strasse muss ich gehen / Die noch keiner ging zurück."*

"That's it?" the young composer sharply replied, annoyed by his friend's evasiveness.

"'From the road that I must take / No one has yet returned.'"

"In other words?"

Lenny just shrugged his shoulders. "*I* understand what I mean."

Iris Nueil was three years my junior, a violinist whose parents objected to people whom they scornfully called "the artists," by which they meant anyone who didn't practice a liberal profession or work as a government official; they strove, therefore, to thwart their daughter's plans. She'd quarreled

---

* From Verlaine's *Sagesse*.

33

with them, moved out of the family apartment in Auteuil, and was currently renting a room as wretched as my own near the Père Lachaise Cemetery. I appreciated her company; Iris was talented—and very beautiful.

"That may be, but I don't understand you at all!" Hermin retorted, a little too curtly.

Spurred by irritation, he quickened his pace, even though they were going uphill. His attempts to engage in conversation had been stymied by the younger man's mutism, and Lenny, on his side, hadn't made the slightest effort. In the end, wasn't Hermin obliged to point out his companion's dodges and evasions?

Though he was a little pale, Lenny started walking faster too, not wanting to fall too far behind. He was about to say something when a fit of coughing stopped and shook him. To allow him time to recover, Hermin slowed down, but instead of abating, Lenny's coughing was coupled with a kind of suffocation. Paler still, his hands clenched into fists against his chest, his breath coming in gasps, Lenny had to support himself against one of the stacks of logs beside the path.

"Lenny...Lenny, are you all right?"

"Yes...no problem..." the boy panted.

His coughing gradually calmed down. He'd shut his eyes.

"Look, if you don't feel like continuing, let's go back. We can skip the Germanies..."

Surprisingly enough, the younger man didn't protest and limited himself to a vague nod. Hermin chided himself: Wasn't what he had just censured as unwillingness actually fatigue?

"Have you caught a cold? Maybe you should see a doctor..."

Lenny gave a smile—a smile, one might have said, of connivance with himself.

"Not worth the trouble..."

If they cut through the woods, Hermin thought, they could get back to the pavilion pretty quickly, and there his friend could recover enough strength to make a final effort and reach the Pommier Chenin.

Lenny said nothing and let me go off to the Conservatory, where Iris and I had arranged to meet; but when I returned that evening, he was still there, waiting for me. Should I have recognized that as a sign of his solitude? I confess to not having gauged, at that moment, the significance of his action.

The younger man approved of the idea and stood up straight, and then the two of them plunged into the underbrush.

4

ARPEGGIONE SONATA

S oon they were able to make out the music pavilion. It was Lenny who first spotted its snow-covered roof through the trees. It surprised him: the white surface seemed to be suspended above the ground, so thoroughly did the structure's dark walls blend in with the surrounding tree trunks, and it was possible to imagine that *Frau Holle's** secret domain lay behind the row of pine trees armed with pikes. Hermin had often thought about those Germanic tales in which the local spirit, the fairy of the place, lures children in order to put them to the test. A mysterious charm seemed to urge hikers on toward the cabin, and Lenny, nourished on fabulous stories about disquieting Ice Maidens busily at work, could not be immune to that charm.

---

* The title of one of *Grimm's Fairy Tales*, known in English as "Mother Holle" or "Mother Hulda" or "Old Mother Frost."

It so happened that I didn't see him for several weeks. Since I had no possible way of reaching him, I decided to wait for a return which, I had no doubt, would eventually take place. I took the opportunity to see Iris again, as well as some other friends; furthermore, I entered a composition contest, submitting a vocal quartet inspired by the first verses of St. John's Gospel and duly titled Flesh and Word. *To my astonishment, I won the prize. I was delighted by this accomplishment, but disappointed at the same time because—and this provided a way of measuring how close the two of us had become—I couldn't share my delight with Lenny. I was forced to surrender to the evidence: I missed the boy.*

As always, dampness had swollen the wooden door, the portal of crudely squared-off planks that guarded the entrance to his sanctuary, and Hermin had to make several attempts to budge the thing before a hard blow from his shoulder did the trick. As he'd done upon arriving at the Pommier Chenin, Lenny remained silent for a long time, peering at the shelves packed with music scores, at the piles of manuscripts on the table, at the boxes overflowing with audiotapes, theoretical studies, and aborted compositions that Hermin, ever since settling into the premises, had never found the nerve to classify. Only after a while did Lenny say, "You are very well here."

The young composer nodded mutely. A period of silence ensued. Then Lenny moved timidly to the worktable and, seeing that his friend was making no effort to stop him, started to pore over the rough scores and sketches heaped up there in the most thorough disorder. Hermin remained where he was. Mechanically, he picked up the latest issue of *Diapason*, which had come in the previous day's mail. "Look here, it's got a review of your last concert," he said, indicating the table of contents, which included an enigmatic title in the young pianist's native language, a reference to both Franz Schubert and Richard Strauss: "*Wieck im Abendrot.*"*

Hermin didn't have time to say anything more. The young man, looking rather pale, practically snatched the magazine from his hands.

Hermin raised his eyebrows. He remembered a rebellious boy who cared little about pleasing others or heeding the advice he received, and he wouldn't have imagined that his young friend could be interested in what music critics had to say at the very moment when he claimed to be abandoning music.

His return was long in coming. In reality, I knew nothing about the boy except his name, Wieck, and as I might have guessed, there was no Wieck listed in the telephone book. On the off chance, I went regularly to the Conservatory and looked for him in the practice studios: in vain. What else to do?

---

* "Wieck at Sunset."

Lenny took a few seconds to run his eyes over the article and tore out the page, which he folded and put in his pocket. Then, as though nothing had interrupted him, he returned his attention to the annotated score he'd started to read through. Hermin, taken aback, stared at him.

"Is it a bad review?"

A strange smile played on the young man's lips, but he didn't bother to raise his head. "Worse than that."

In the end, the boy made his reappearance in the piano store, looking and acting much as he'd done the first time: hesitant, intimidated. Although we were in the month of December, he wasn't wearing a coat, and he was shivering in his inevitable wool sweater. I quickly went over to him; his cheeks had grown gaunt since our last meeting, and he'd lost weight.

"But...come on, Lenny, what does the review say?" Hermin asked haltingly.

"Things you know. It says that after the concert, I explained that I am canceling all the others..."

"Lenny, you can't be serious. Let me read it."

"*Nein!*"

The syllable had rung out in the pavilion, and Lenny's involuntary recourse to German was sufficient proof of how genuine his refusal was. Hermin looked at him; it wasn't his former protégé he saw standing in front of him, but a stranger.

"Are you ill?" I asked, suddenly worried.

"No, I am not," he said, avoiding me.

His voice was a little hoarse.

The young man had dived back into the score he'd been reading. As on the evening of their reunion, Hermin observed him on the sly. After a week of cohabitation, Hermin still hadn't penetrated any of the secrets his friend seemed to wallow in. But after all, that was the way he'd always been. Even when they were both ten years younger, the boy had remained silent as long as possible on the subject of what went on in his life besides piano lessons, and he'd confided in Hermin only when necessity had left him no other choice. Furthermore, the young composer suddenly thought, strange though it was that Lenny hadn't offered any explanation of his decision to return after such a long absence, it was stranger still that he had provided no retrospective justification for his sudden disappearance ten years before—as though, despite the passage of so many years, the information still couldn't be declassified. Maybe it was up to Hermin to ask the questions, but he didn't dare. Over the course of their relationship, which had been stormy to say the least, Hermin had learned that the most trivial misjudged word, the smallest inappropriate question, could set off a cataclysm. In short, Lenny, by so often remaining mute, had gradually constrained Hermin to keep his own mouth shut. This reciprocal silence had most assuredly led, ten years ago, to incomprehension followed by separation, and now incomprehension, deepened by absence, was the cause of the present muteness...

As I was about to ask him what he intended to do there, the shop bell tinkled and two customers entered—an extremely rare occurrence—to try out the pianos. During a long half hour, I had to devote my attention to the newcomers, rattle off the characteristics of the different Steinways, compare the advantages of the Mag and the Blüthner, and—supreme torture—endure the opening bars of that tedious chestnut, Mozart's "Turkish March," played on every keyboard in the place. I was seething.

Absorbed in these reflections, Hermin hadn't realized that he'd continued to stare fixedly at Lenny, and he got flustered when the young man raised his head and their eyes met. There was a moment of embarrassment, and they confusedly sensed that one of them *had* to say something, for the law of discretion had always governed their relationship, and this infringement must be conjured away, fast. Hermin tossed out the first remark that came to his mind while he opportunely shifted his gaze to the window. "It's going to start snowing soon, we shouldn't let ourselves get snowed in here..."

Lenny played dumb and asked, with a tentative smile, "Can we not stay a little while longer? It is so nice here, in your cabin..."

Hermin gestured vaguely. He couldn't care less about atmospheric disturbances, and to tell the truth, he wasn't at all sure that it would start snowing before nightfall. His young companion stayed quiet for a few moments before going on without looking at him, as though fearing a refusal: "Since we are here...could you talk to me about your compositions? You have not told me anything about them..."

"I could say much the same thing to you. You haven't been exactly chatty on the subject of your career."

Nor on any other subject whatsoever, Hermin thought, but he kept it to himself. By imperceptible degrees, Lenny's shoulders tensed up. At last he replied, "That is different. There is nothing to say, I swear."

"You must be kidding me! Lenny, you've played all over, you've met the greatest—"

"You see, you already know everything from *Diapason* and France Musique. What could I add?"

"Come on, there's a limit to what journalists can come up with! Your take is surely different from theirs! And... where you're concerned, I have the right to know a bit more than the average music lover, don't I?"

The couple left the store, still undecided, and as soon as they were outside, I hung the "Back in a few minutes" sign on the door and pulled Lenny into the room in the rear of the shop. "Well?" I said. "What's going on?"

Hermin saw Lenny bite his lips and understood that he'd hit home. "What is it you want to know, exactly?" the boy asked after a while, his gaze obstinately fixed on the garlands of frost that festooned the window.

"Well, for example, I've always wondered...Why haven't you taken the opportunity to record the *Transcendental Études*? You worked and worked on them..."

"Does not matter if I did. Everybody does that when they are twenty, because you have to prove you are a real musician, a virtuoso..."

"Exactly, so with the Liszt, you would have proved that better than anyone, wouldn't you?"

"But I did not want to prove anything. I was there, that is all. What I hate is...Now a pianist is asked only to be— how do you say that again?—photogenic, just so, photogenic, and able to play 'Mazeppa' without problems..."

Lenny satisfied both of those requirements; maybe he wasn't aware of it, but they had served him better than anyone else. To sum up, Hermin thought, the others play the *Transcendentals* out of pride, and in order to outbid their pride, Lenny doesn't play them, period. It was as though Hermin had just shined a new light on his young friend's refusal to go on performing: Could that also be attributed to his pride, to his desire for the absolute? At the age of twenty-seven, he was one of the best pianists of his generation, and he knew it. To choose silence—was that not to remove the risk of any fall? Every year, new virtuosos are launched onto the music market. The fame of the pianist called "the Wanderer" was certainly solid, but as always in artistic circles, it was never definitively assured. So the choice of silence made him, in a way, the piano world's equivalent of Rimbaud—a living myth. Had he deliberately sought to create his own legend? Hermin rejected that idea: what he knew about his friend had nothing in common with such an unflattering portrait. Lenny wasn't one of those whose love of music subsides once success is achieved. And yet, there was one element that seemed to invalidate this hypothesis: the review, which the young man had indicated was unfavorable. Perhaps, then, a concert that "bombed"—such as all musicians have suffered through—had wounded Lenny's pride so deeply that he'd decided to give it up, all of it, in a gesture that was so very much like him…For the lad was and had always been an adept at *all-or-nothing*; Hermin had often been obliged to suffer the repercussions of that trait.

"Am I…am I a good pianist?"

The question, which had no apparent connection to what he'd just been saying, disconcerted me. "Well…" I said. "You still have work to do, but don't doubt for one second that you're going to be an exceptional musician."

"So," he went on, without looking at me, "will I be able to give a concert soon?"

A concert? I was flabbergasted. Where, how, with whose help?

"I need money."

The young composer shook his head to chase away those thoughts and returned his attention to his young friend, who, for a change, was deigning to reply to his questions!

"Your first prize at the Marguerite Long Competition—can you tell me about that?"

Lenny shrugged. "There is nothing to tell. I was the youngest contestant, that was why they gave me the prize."

"But afterward, you met Brendel, Fischer-Dieskau, and especially the Maestro…"

"The Maestro, I saw him only three times."

"That's quite a lot!"

Lenny smiled at last and raised his head. "Maybe so. Once he told me he really liked my 'last sonatas,' but if Schubert had not existed, that would not have changed any thing in the history of music!"

"Yes, he likes to land that particular blow. I've heard him say it before."

"I said that Schubert's music is beautiful, and nothing better has been composed since."

"Lenny!" the composer exclaimed, in a scandalized tone that failed to hide his amusement. That impudence, so charming in the teenage boy, that pleasure in overstepping limits, had obviously been maintained after their separation…

"I think he took it badly. There was a project in the works, he and I were going to record Liszt's concertos together, but in the end it did not happen."*

"Well, you know, those bratty little insinuations of yours, I would have taken them badly too!"

"But your music is beautiful!"

The young composer raised his eyebrows. "You don't know it! It has nothing to do with what I was writing when you were studying with me...that pseudo-avant-garde stuff everybody expected of us..."

Lenny's cheeks flushed slightly. "I know that. I am a little familiar with the contemporary music milieu. Philippe Hersant showed me the score of your *De profundis* for contralto and chamber orchestra, and last year they performed your *Todesfuge*† in the auditorium of the Nice Conservatory. In fact, every time there has been a concert of your work and you were not there, I managed to catch it..."

Hermin stared at his friend. "You want to organize your first concert and sell tickets for it, but nobody has heard you yet!"

"I have no choice!"

He had almost shouted. His voice cracked in a way that made me realize his demand wasn't at all capricious.

---

* The project would later be realized with Daniel Barenboim as the piano soloist.

† "Death Fugue," a poem by Paul Celan.

"But you, you've never come to hear me," the younger man said, turning his eyes away. "In the Schubert Year...I was invited to Vienna for the bicentenary concert. But I stayed in Paris, hoping you would be at the Salle Pleyel."

"I always buy your records as soon as they come out," Hermin said, defending himself. Lenny raised his head. A bright, fleeting gleam lit up his dark eyes, and then in a voice that strove to sound neutral, he asked, "So what did you think?"

The young composer remained silent for a few moments. What to say? That he'd listened to the Brahms *Intermezzi* until he was exhausted, that he'd made the Pommier Chenin's walls resound with the *Années de Pèlerinage* and nothing else for months?

"I loved your Liszt. A lot."

Lenny nodded.

"Although maybe you do take 'Le Mal du pays' a little too fast...And I wonder if the 'Vallée d'Obermann' doesn't deserve more rubato. But those are only details..."

Precisely: details. In spite of himself, he'd just revealed his perfect knowledge of his young friend's recordings. Lenny smiled, barely.

"That is not what you said about 'Obermann' before! You used to say the opposite!"

Obviously, Hermin wasn't the only one who'd kept in his memory everything that had to do with the *other*...

After a moment of hesitation, I invited him to sit on an old piano bench that had been demoted to the back of the shop months previously. I drew up a chair. I resumed talking, more gently this time: "Explain it to me from the beginning. So you want to make some money by giving a concert."

He nodded.

"And you can't get this money any other way?"

The opposite of a nod to indicate no. *His disappearance had clearly failed to make him any more talkative.*

A painful feeling of impotence suddenly overwhelmed Hermin. There they were, then, face-to-face, each of them trying to pierce the veil that separated them, without succeeding, without even daring to make a decisive move, timorous as they were, the two of them. And the understanding they both secretly aspired to couldn't become reality— chiefly through Lenny's fault, Hermin sensed that, but also through the fault of their past, which was too heavy with memories at once happy and unhappy. Once again, he felt torn between his desire to interrogate the young man, to back him up against the wall, and the fear of facing a new refusal. In spite of himself, his frustration began to turn into resentment.

"Good. Now, do you suppose you might explain to me why you need money?" I asked him, divided between annoyance and compassion.

He bit his lip. Once again, his eyes shifted to the right to avoid meeting mine. "I must?"

"If you want me to understand anything about you and your background, yes."

He lowered his head and then raised it toward me, as though he couldn't decide. Then I saw him clench his fists. He looked resolute.

"After all that, you still haven't answered my question," the lad said shyly.

"What question?"

"Could you talk to me about your compositions?"

Hermin permitted himself a mocking smile, and, imitating his friend, accent and all, he said, "You already know everything, thanks to Philippe Hersant and the concert in Nice. What could I add?"

Lenny's face reddened again, but he made a valiant effort to plead his cause. "Right from the start, from the first evening, you did not want to say anything…"

With an irony shading into bitterness, the young composer thought about how very many of his colleagues would have given everything so that such a *personage* as Leonard Wieck would deign to take an interest in their work… Then he said, "I can sum it up in two sentences, if you insist. Let's see…For a year, I worked in a music publishing house, and then I spent eighteen months in Rome as an artist-in-residence in the Villa Medici. I went back to Paris, and the following year I moved here. You see, not exactly novel material!"

"How was the Villa? Nice?"

"Pretty nice. I didn't write much, but I met other composers, like Éric Tanguy and Stefano Gervasoni, interesting guys... In fact, the three of us quickly formed a sort of trio, even though our approaches are different..."

Lenny nodded and chose not to ask any other questions.

"My aunt is sick. We do not have money. So I am trying to earn some."

"You live with her? You...you don't have your parents?"

"No."

I began to get a glimpse into Lenny's situation—and to understand why he'd dropped out of sight.

"If I ask you some other questions, will you answer them?"

"Depends. When I can."

"How long has your aunt been ill?"

"A long time. Ever since...we arrived in Paris. She is worse now, because of the winter."

"You spend all your time taking care of her?"

"Yes. Except when I work with you."

So now I'd received—in passing—confirmation that he didn't attend any high school.

Perhaps the worst for the young composer was the thought that he'd lived and labored so hard for ten years in order to reach that particular day, that precise scene. How many times had he imagined Lenny leaning over his shoulder to read his scores, suggesting a few alterations or, even better, sitting down at the piano to sight-read his latest works! And now the hour had come, the one he'd imagined as a lustral water that would purify them when they met again, and instead the hour was clouded, even tainted, by their old enemies: reticence, incomprehension, stubbornness.

"And…if this isn't an indiscreet question, what's she suffering from?"

He cast his eyes down. "I do not know the French word. I think it is Lungenkrankheit *in German…"*

"Which doesn't help me any," I pointed out.

There followed a period of silence.

Hermin couldn't keep pretending to observe the landscape through the window. He turned around, repressing a sigh, and gave himself some cover by starting to search his shelves for the score of Schubert's Arpeggione Sonata. He needed that score for his project, but so far he hadn't been able to put his hand on it. Let's see, where hadn't he looked yet? There were so many stacks of boxes here and there, containers whose contents he had never got around to shelving…More or less at random, he started to rummage in one such box and extracted from it material related to various old Conservatory courses, some pay stubs, and the addresses of Parisian luthiers.

"You think this is the moment to tidy up?" Lenny asked from behind him, his voice a little sardonic.

Hermin didn't bother to reply, limiting himself to a shrug. After having put everything back in a jumble, he moved to another box, this one filled with audiotapes and cassettes he'd recorded himself in the days of his stereophonic endeavors. No chance that the Arpeggione would be in there... He was about to give up when a black cassette tape caught his attention. There was nothing written on the outside of the box, but on the inside, in uppercase, slightly shaky letters, he saw the name: LENNY.

Gripped by an emotion that nothing justified, he leapt to his feet, the cassette in his hand, and spoke excitedly to his young friend. "Lenny, do you know what this is?"

He seemed to see the youth gradually stiffen before answering, in a voice perhaps less resonant than usual, "I did not think I left any recordings."

Hermin had forgotten; when Lenny fled, he'd taken with him some scores annotated in his friend's hand as well as tapes of their lessons and of his own first concert. So had one of those tapes been inadvertently forgotten?

"We could listen to it this evening..."

The young man made no sign to indicate either acceptance or refusal of this proposal; Hermin took silence for acquiescence and put the cassette in his pocket.

So what could I do for Lenny? I found his concert project impracticable, for at least two reasons: the first was that I couldn't see myself, a simple student, organizing a recital for a boy nobody had ever heard of; the second was that I was under no delusion, I knew I was a very inadequate piano teacher, and I was not unaware that Lenny, however great his natural talent, still had progress to make before he could perform on a stage. That being the case, what could I come up with as an alternative?

He turned back to his shelves, intent on making one last effort to find the Arpeggione Sonata, the score he was interested in. Schoenberg, Schubert, Schumann…after all, he wouldn't have put it anywhere else! And yet the only works in the Schubert section he'd already checked—were trios and quartets. He looked once again, of course, and of course the Arpeggione was still not there…He could see it, that score, a blue urtext edition whose cover curled upward at the corners…Let's see, he wondered, how long had it been since he'd studied that piece? A long time, a very long time… Now that he thought about it, it was quite possible that the score had stayed in Paris; in the moving process, he had shed many belongings, and then two boxes had been lost, a real disaster…But for the most part it was Berg and Berio who had disappeared, along with a bit of Boulez, whereas Brahms had, by pure chance, arrived safe and sound…His mind was wandering; Schubert had nothing to do with any of that…

Unless…Hadn't he recently remembered that when Lenny left the garret room, he'd taken a few scores with him? Could the Arpeggione have been one of them? He should ask him…although he would surely not bother to reply…With a brusque movement, the young composer dropped a pile of old sketches back onto his worktable and gave up his search.

The composition contest I'd won years ago flashed into my mind, the victory I'd wanted to tell Lenny about, had I had any idea how to reach him. The prize had included a fine ceremony amid the gilded splendor of the Hôtel de Ville in Paris as well as a goodly sum of money that I'd planned to spend on a new bow and some scores. However, couldn't I imagine another use for it?

"Lenny…maybe I've got another solution for you."

"Do you remember the scores you took from the garret?"

The young man, who was leafing through a treatise on harmony, froze. "Yes," he said in a neutral voice. "Of course."

"I've been looking for the Arpeggione for several days now."

Lenny's cheeks flushed slightly. "I have it. I have all those scores, in fact…they are in my bag."

Hermin couldn't hold back a movement of surprise. The lad had arrived at the Pommier Chenin practically empty-handed, but he had in his baggage a half-dozen scores he'd purloined ten years before!

"But...why burden yourself with them if you have no intention of working?"

Lenny's blush deepened and he shrugged his shoulders, looking embarrassed. "I do not know."

The lie was too obvious for Hermin even to think about voicing the least objection, so he chose to pivot to another idea that had just occurred to him: "That sonata...I remember you liked it a lot...Why haven't you ever recorded it?"

"What would be your guess?"

The young composer, surprised by this reply and by the bitter tone it had been couched in, made a gesture of ignorance. "How should I know?" he asked. "You must be acquainted with any number of cellists who would have been glad to play it with you—"

"The only person I wanted to play it with was Hermin Peyre."

The interruption took the young composer by surprise. It was true that the Arpeggione Sonata had been "the national anthem of their friendship," and for good reason: with the piano and cello—it didn't matter that the cello part had been conceived for another instrument—bound together over the course of several sublime pages, from the sweetly melancholy first movement to the ardent third, the piece offered quite enough material to impassion the two players…And besides, wasn't the Arpeggione Sonata the only one of Schubert's duets that could be included in a cellist's repertoire? A work dedicated to the two of them from all eternity…

"In that case, why don't we start working on it together again?"

He raised his head and looked at me. His face was full of hope. If my decision hadn't already been made, I would have made it at that moment. I'd never been able to resist Lenny, with his lost-child looks and his changing gaze, sometimes provocative, sometimes imploring.

"You know, I won a composition contest…"

"Wie schön!"*

He seemed genuinely happy to hear about my success, and I was touched.

"I don't need the check they gave me," I went on, not without a pang in my heart for the bow I'd coveted in a luthier's shop a few days previously. "Take it."

The young man, who was still examining the shelves of musical scores, turned around. His lips were trembling. He shot Hermin a distraught glance and for some seconds seemed to be engaged in a violent internal combat. At last, he clenched his fists and said, "Not now, not anymore. Besides…"

---

* "That's great!"

"Besides what?" Hermin asked.

But Lenny only shrugged. Hermin hesitated briefly and then plunged ahead: "Lenny, if you're wondering why I'm making notes on these Schubert scores, it's because I'm composing a piece based on quotations from his works. It's probably going to be for a piano trio, or maybe for a quintet, echoing the *Trout*. In any case, I'm going to need a pianist—a good pianist—if I want to perform the piece one day. I can't imagine anyone but you interpreting it."

Once again, they gazed at each other in silence. The youth had always had the eyes of a drowning man trying in vain to escape his fate. Without wanting to admit it to himself, Hermin thought that Lenny's distracted look was as beautiful as any smile.

"Hermin..." the boy finally murmured, "if it was just a question of doing you a favor, I would say yes. But I cannot..."

A bitter taste rose in the young composer's throat; sure, he'd foreseen such a reply, but this fresh failure seemed particularly cruel, considering his feeling that Lenny could easily have accepted the proposal, and that the reasons for his refusal were now, if anything, even more obscure. And besides...he knew nothing of the sort would have happened had their situations been reversed: he'd always given in to Lenny, and Lenny had never given in to him. Once again, resentment overcame him. He could have bickered, could have argued; but he lacked the strength for that, and so he moved, discouraged, to the window.

I had expected him to demonstrate how happy my offer made him, but he did nothing of the sort.

"I could not pay you back...and so I cannot accept."

I started laughing. "If you insist," I said, "you can always repay me after you become a famous pianist and get your picture on the cover of Diapason*..."*

He gave me a pallid smile, but he didn't look persuaded.

That was when he saw it coming: the snow was beginning to flutter down in barely perceptible flakes; it was difficult to believe they would succeed all by themselves in transforming the entire landscape—but as Hermin well knew, they would manage the job in just a few hours. Behind him, the young man coughed a little.

"Come on," I persisted, *"you're welcome to it, I assure you. You need it more than I do."*

He remained silent for a moment, no doubt weighing the pros and cons. Eventually, he nodded assent.

A moment later, they were hurrying down the slope that led to the Pommier Chenin.

5

FANTASIA IN F MINOR

B reathless, they sank into the armchairs in the Great
Room. While Lenny, shaken by a new coughing fit,
gasped for air, Hermin began a feverish search for a
subject, any subject, capable of guaranteeing a *normal* conversation. The silence must not be allowed to drag on and on
again; topics of an oversensitive nature must not be brought
up…Suddenly, he felt an object in his pants pocket—the
cassette he'd found a short time before—and he was saved;
they needed only to listen to it.

He showed the object to Lenny and said, "All right with
you if we see what this is?"

"If you want…" Lenny replied, shrugging his shoulders.

Without waiting for any further comment, the young
composer inserted the cassette in the player. A disturbing

crackling sound issued from the speakers. "The humidity hasn't done it any good…"

The static stopped; notes could be heard.

The memory came back to Hermin immediately: a rehearsal of Schubert's Fantasia in F minor, a piece for four hands that he and Lenny had started to work on before eventually abandoning the effort. In the last months of his life, Schubert lived with his friend Schober, and Hermin had always wondered whether that fact hadn't given rise to the late outpouring of works for four hands—the Fantasia, an Allegro, a Rondo, a Fugue—in a sort of amicable communion that functioned as a substitute for the pipe dream of a romantic collaboration.

We would play music together in the garret, sitting side by side on the threadbare velvet of the old piano bench, which creaked and groaned with every movement we made; our shoulders would touch, and so would our legs. Without regret, I'd let Lenny take the high part, which he exalted with his singing sound, by turns sorrowful, violent, thin, panting; as for me, I provided muted accompaniment, trying to disguise, as best I could, my deficiencies: I hadn't done much work on the piece and didn't possess the instantaneous sight-reading ability, no doubt innate in the greatest players, of which Lenny gave daily, dazzling proof. Nonetheless, I used to love playing with him…

"I used to love playing with you," the young man suddenly said, his voice toneless, his eyes fixed on the window adorned with frost. "Yes, I used to love that…"

"We could start again—it's up to you. I'm ready."

Lenny raised his head. For an instant, the light that enlivened his pupils thrust into Hermin's eyes like a lance piercing a breastplate. Then, just as rapidly, he turned away.

"Let us not talk about it. You must not insist…"

Then he stopped speaking. The development of Schubert's theme, now in a major key, was proceeding apace, and the melody, Hermin's skirmishing in the bass register, the tape hiss in the cassette, and their twinned breathing resounded indiscriminately in the room.

"Do you hear?" Lenny went on when their eyes met again.

The question might have seemed strange; however, from the young man's intonation, from his furtive glance, Hermin understood, beyond any possibility of error, what Lenny was alluding to. He himself hadn't stopped paying attention to it, not since the very start. Their mingled breathing functioned as a sort of symbol for their former connection, for what united them back then, for the bond to which the young composer today hesitated to give the beautiful name of friendship, although he could think of no more fitting term.

"You can hear Gould breathing too, in his recording of the *Goldbergs*," Hermin said. "You can even hear him singing," he added in a strangled voice, well aware that Lenny wouldn't be fooled by these beside-the-point reflections.

Suddenly, their listening to that cassette together seemed oddly reckless to Hermin. It was better not to exhume certain buried emotions.

"I know…but that is not exactly what I mean…Does not matter anyhow."

At the same instant, ten years earlier, they attacked a forte passage; Lenny was faultlessly executing chords and broken arpeggios, while Hermin was wrestling with the particularly convoluted accompaniment. Soon he settled for playing the theme in the bass, more or less in time. Suddenly, Lenny's voice, hardly distorted at all, erupted from the speakers, crying out in a tone full of reproach: "*Hermin!*"

Back then, Lenny's accent was still quite heavy, and he pronounced his friend's name almost as *Herman*, a mistake that amused Hermin.

"*Hermin! You are spoiling the best passage!*"

"*I'm doing the best I can!*"

Hermin recalled the scene. In an incredible effort, he'd tried and succeeded—for three measures—to play all the notes with his right hand before realizing that by doing so he'd slowed down, with the result that he and Lenny were out of sync. Discouraged, Hermin had stopped altogether.

"Hermin! Why?"

"Turn it off," twenty-seven-year-old Lenny said in a low voice. He was clenching his fists so hard that his knuckles had turned white and his fingernails were digging into his flesh. "Now I remember that day. We had an argument. I do not feel like listening to that."

But Hermin, strangely fascinated by those voices risen from the past, didn't stop the tape.

"Forgive me... We're not at the same level anymore, and you know it!"

"That is not important. Once more, from the beginning of the forte..."

"It's no use. Look, Lenny, you're going to have to get used to this idea: we can't play together anymore...I can sight-read simpler things, but this..."

"You can do anything if you work at it. Let us try it again, Hermin..."

His voice was practically pleading when he said Hermin's name.

And his eyes likewise, ten years later, imploring Hermin to stop the cassette.

"No. Lenny, we may as well have this out once and for all. I've tried my best to help you progress, but now there's *nothing more I can do for you... If you want to make the piano your profession, you need to be taught by a master. With me, you're picking up bad habits. I'm holding you back more than helping you!"*

"Even if that is true... it does not mean we cannot play together!"

"I can't just play this piece at the drop of a hat—I'd have to work on it for hours and hours—and I don't have the time! What would you say if I handed you my cello and demanded we play a sonata together?"

"Maybe I could not do it, but I would try!"

"Oh, stop. In any case, I have to go out. If you insist, we can take up the piece again another day..."

Lenny got up. "You like listening to this?" he asked harshly, almost aggressively. "I should have known... You liked it when we argued..."

"The hell I did!"

"You liked it, I tell you! For me, every argument was pain, but you, you loved that, admit it, you loved our ugly cat-and-dog fights!"

Hermin, wounded by those words—whose justice he was able to glimpse—didn't answer and went back to listening. During the few seconds when they'd stopped paying attention to the recording, their conversation had grown remarkably heated.

"Go ahead, I do not care!" Lenny cried.

"Please…let's be reasonable, let's not get all upset for nothing…"

"I do not feel like being reasonable! Hermin…I thought you liked working with me…But I was wrong, I sure was! I am the 'boy wonder' you want to launch for your own glory… You could not care less if we play together or not!"

"You don't know what you're talking about!"

They heard Lenny burst into bitter laughter.

"Oh, yes I do! Hermin Peyre, the great discoverer…I am sure it is the same for Iris too, and for others I do not know…So look, tell me, how many discoveries did you make before me?"

"Lenny, you're crazy!"

"I hope you're not still stuck on that idea," Hermin broke in, bewildered.

The beginning of a smile appeared on Lenny's lips. "I was angry, I did not really think that…Actually, I do not know…"

"Lenny!" Hermin exclaimed.

But he was interrupted by the sound of a slap that echoed across the years.

"Who hit who?" he wondered, in an almost inaudible voice.

"You slapped me," Lenny answered.

A slamming door resounded in its turn.

"That was me leaving, no doubt," Hermin murmured.

Lenny agreed, biting his lip. The young composer saw him move to stop the tape and grabbed him by the wrist. For a moment, they struggled in silence. In defiance of all logic, Hermin was determined to listen to the recording all the way to the end.

Ten years before, alone in Hermin's garret, Lenny was crying. For a few seconds, they listened to his sobs. The young man had given up the idea of turning off the cassette.

Then silence fell—either because teenage Lenny had thought to stop the tape, or because the tape had run out on its own.

They looked at each other, ashen-faced. Before that evening, Hermin had never imagined that Lenny could cry.

"Do you remember that?" Hermin asked.

The young man didn't respond; any response would be useless.

After a pause, he asked hoarsely, "Can I see the cassette?"

Without a word, Hermin ejected the tape, removed it, and handed it over. Lenny held it in the palm of his hand. He remained unmoving for an instant, standing upright, his face illuminated by the flames, which bent like grasses in a big wind. Then, abruptly, he made a movement, his arm remained suspended a moment—Hermin repressed a cry—the cassette was already in the fire.

6

SERENADE

O ver the course of several days, a wind heavily laden with snow blew continuously. Winter had brusquely taken up residence, but neither Hermin nor Lenny, each of them too busy conducting mutual surveillance and pondering the other's words like so many encrypted messages, had noticed. Relentless gusts battered the Pommier Chenin; the old dwelling screeched, moaned, and trembled under the tempest's blows. The shipwreck-like commotion was augmented by the sound of Lenny's footsteps as he wandered around the house the way he would have roamed the countryside, alone, aimless, staring into space. To avoid running into him around the corner of a corridor, Hermin took refuge in his room, almost as lethargic as the person whose idleness he shunned. He went, without enthusiasm, from his cello to his records, played a few pieces, gave up on them; most of the time he wound up falling inertly onto his bed. Although he wouldn't have admitted it, the Schubertian hammering of his guest's footsteps had at least the merit of giving a rhythm to days otherwise devoid of meaning. When a brief lull provided an opportunity, the boy would take off, hiking the Montagne Bourbonnaise, while Hermin went back to his pavilion for some halfhearted work. In general, they both returned to the Pommier Chenin at nightfall and had dinner in silence before retiring to their respective rooms. Life weighed heavily on them.

Although our relations had become less formal, numerous shadowy areas remained. I still knew little about his life, and I hardly ever tried to overcome his habitual silence. Nonetheless, certain phrases, certain words escaped him, and they confirmed the impression he gave of an almost total solitude; the assiduousness he demonstrated was, no doubt, as much a proof of his growing love for music as of his odd attachment to me—one of the only people, apparently, who associated with him and tried to understand him.

One evening when he'd stayed late in his music pavilion, Hermin was obliged to tear himself from his work in a hurry. He hadn't noticed how the time was passing, but the sky, already partly dark and heavy with snow, clearly indicated that he'd better get back to the main house quickly if he didn't want to spend the night snowed in. Lenny, he thought,

must already be back and starting to get worried about him...
Hermin quickly gathered up the sketches strewn over his
desk, jogged them into a rough stack, grabbed a few scores he
wanted to read at his leisure, and left the pavilion.

But when he arrived at the Pommier Chenin, the house
was still empty. Lenny, apparently, had also stayed out
too late. Worried, the young composer took a fresh look at
the sky through the window, and what he saw made him
grimace.

That was when he noticed a scrap of paper lying con-
spicuously on the table.

"I am off to see the Pierre Charbonnière. That name
tempted me since I read it on your regional maps. I am not
really sure how much time it takes, but I hope before night
to be back. See you later, then. Lenny."

Hermin turned the young man's message over and over
between his fingers. He pondered it for a good while: the awkward syntax, the chicken-scratch penmanship, the willfully
long strokes, the way Lenny formed his capitals, his signa-
ture. Despite their two years together, Hermin had, practically speaking, never read anything the boy had written,
except for the very rare annotations that he made on scores,
which, since they indicated fingering, didn't really offer much
of a handwriting sample. Not without some bitterness, he
thought about the message Lenny had refused to leave him
when he ran away, and about the letters he'd waited for, letters

that obviously had never been written. Did those lost words have to be replaced, however futilely, by the few sentences of the present note? Perhaps Lenny had realized, at least in part, the mistakes that had caused their split and had resolved to follow another path...Improbable as this hypothesis might be as applied to the current state of their relationship—silence, misunderstandings, latent disappointment—Hermin seized on it with the strength of a shipwrecked man clinging to a miraculous raft. And, victimized by an exaggerated attachment that he himself found annoying but which he was unable to resist, he thrust the note into his pocket.

One day, I got the idea of introducing him to Iris. I had a confused notion that their meeting would serve to soften the mute hostility he displayed whenever I left him to spend time with my friends. The vocal performance majors were giving a recital at the Conservatory, and I invited Lenny to attend it with us—Iris for her part had gladly accepted the invitation—thinking that he'd be delighted to meet some real musicians at last; but when I proposed the outing to him, he bit his lip, shook his head, and replied only that he couldn't come. I was disappointed; I suggested that he could join us in the afternoon and stay with us until the concert, which was set to begin at seven o'clock; he accepted.

He went over to the hearth, poked at the embers, revived the fire, and added a few logs. Chilled by several hours of composition in his pavilion, he took comfort from the blaze for a few seconds, holding his hands very close to the flames. Curling up in an armchair, watching the evening come down on the snowy landscape, and listening to Hans Hotter's performance of *Winterreise* while distractedly reading Robert and Clara Schumann's joint diary amounted to one of the greatest pleasures that winter provided him. However, on that particular evening, Lenny's absence and the necessity of waiting for him until nightfall spoiled the prospect of such pleasure like a streak of mud across snow.

On the appointed day, we—Iris, Lenny, and I—met at a café in the neighborhood. I introduced the two of them; the boy spoke very little, but he was habitually taciturn, and I'd warned Iris about that so she wouldn't take offense at his apparently frosty demeanor—which was essentially due, I thought, to shyness.

Anxiety was already tormenting him. The image of the young man trapped in the snow while descending from the Pierre Charbonnière invaded Hermin's brain for a few seconds. He strove, without complete success, to cancel the mental picture and then began to pace despondently up and down the room. The thought of Lenny wouldn't leave him, but little by little it took on a completely different cast. That wasn't unusual in those days, when his mind oscillated like the pendulum of a grandfather clock between two images he couldn't manage to blend into each other: that of teenage Lenny, and that of the semi-stranger he was presently harboring under his roof. And so Hermin passed from disquiet to a reverie of mingled regret and nostalgia for the years of their youth.

I can't remember with any certainty what the topics of our conversation were. No doubt we discussed music news before turning to Conservatory gossip. Somewhere in the middle of a sentence, Iris mentioned her parents and their life in Auteuil; Lenny sat up straight and asked her, almost aggressively, if she lived with them. She told him about their differences, and he nodded pensively.

Hermin sat at the Zimmermann and picked out a few notes that echoed like a call in the silent room—a call to which, as he knew, Lenny would have barely paid attention, even if he'd heard it. How many times had Hermin waited, hoping in vain that the boy's inclination would jibe with his own wishes...

Time passed. We were comfortable in the smoky little café, which protected us from the biting cold, and I was surprised to discover how long we'd stayed there. "It's almost six-thirty! We have to go..."

Iris nodded and seized her purse. Lenny had turned pale. "Six-thirty!" he repeated in a strangled voice.

However, the melody he was more or less randomly playing reminded him of a beloved lied, Schubert's "Ständchen," his "Serenade," whose haunting theme had pursued him in the days following Lenny's flight. Mentally, he hummed the tune:

Leise flehen meine Lieder
Durch die Nacht zu dir;
In den stillen Hain hernieder,
Liebchen, komm zu mir!*

And it seemed to him that he heard, inside his head, the sustained accompaniment in staccato chords, and then, phrase after phrase, the somewhat distant response of a piano whose sotto voce song, he thought, echoed the poet's entreaty. He had himself so often played that song of desire, in its transcription for cello...

Fancying that the initial chords of "Ständchen," in the somber key of D minor, would fittingly open his *Homage*, Hermin took Brigitte Massin's general survey of Schubert's works down from its shelf and started looking in the section devoted to *Schwanengesang* for the musicologist's analysis of the lied.

"What's the matter?" I asked.

"I have got an appointment at seven o'clock...the doctor..."

He clearly didn't want to say anything more in front of Iris, but those words sufficed for me. He bit his lip and looked at me, turning red. "I will never make it on time. Unless..."

His effort to find, among the tome's thousand pages, the paragraph concerning Schubert's "Serenade" didn't last

---

* "Hear my songs, so softly pleading / Through the night to thee; / In the dark and silent thicket, / Darling, come to me!"

long. During the time of their living together, he and Lenny had devoured the volume, annotated it, and stuffed it with bookmarks—simple scraps of paper, pieces torn from Hermin's sketches, wildflowers gathered during walks in the woods, bar bills—and the page with the few lines devoted to the song was indicated by one of those markers: a faded photograph. The young composer pounced on it, abandoning Massin's prose.

There were three of them in the snapshot, striking poses before the lens. With a pang in his heart, Hermin lingered a few seconds over the inscrutable smile of the sixteen-year-old boy called Lenny and then turned to his own image, but his gaze was quickly magnetized by the figure standing beside them: Iris.

I looked at him and understood. Yes, I could go with him. I knew Paris much better than he did; I could take shortcuts and prevent him from getting lost somewhere between rue de Madrid and Les Lilas. This was, obviously, the best solution.

The photo must have been taken in winter; the young lady was wearing an elegantly tailored overcoat, a thick white scarf, and a knit cap over a cascade of chestnut hair. Under one arm she held a score, the title clearly legible: one of Kreisler's études. She was laughing.

Iris shot him a look that was anything but amiable. Apparently, she too had understood.

"Where do you live, exactly?"

Lenny turned red again and murmured an address on rue Floréal.

"But that's on the other end of the city!" the girl exclaimed.

Then, turning to me: "Hermin, you can't do this, you'll miss the entire concert…"

"You can sit with Anton and Pierre. I'll be back in time for the interval."

Given the stormy relationship that had existed between Hermin's two companions in the snapshot, looking at it gave him an odd sensation. He checked the back for a date and found one. It was from the early days of their acquaintance, before Iris and Lenny settled into mutual loathing and began to do whatever they could, each of them, to discredit the other in the eyes of their friend.

Hermin sighed, put the photograph on the piano, and looked away. The words of the "Serenade," however, came floating back into his thoughts, insistently, as if giving him a sign.

They grasp the bosom's longing,
They know the pain of love

Night was starting to fall, and likewise snow. Gradually the room grew dimmer, barely saved from the encroaching darkness by the flickering flames. Hermin gave no thought to further illumination, so completely did the half light suit his troubled state of mind. Black blotches floated on the patinated surfaces of the furniture, gradually covering the floor tiles like water flooding previously emergent lands. The Zimmermann's ivory keys glowed unhealthily in the gloom. With an abrupt gesture, he closed the piano, and the resulting sharp little crack echoed in his ears for a long time. And exasperated him, the way the buzzing of flies in summer could be exasperating, or the slow tick-tock of the clock, marking out the seconds like a metronome. The pitiless countdown, the tallying of time, became all too trying in a room that was from now on fully dedicated to waiting. For a moment the young composer thought about stopping the clock, but then he scoffed at such a ridiculous idea. Time kept on passing.

One companion greeted my resolution with relief, and the other with barely concealed resentment. We did as I suggested. I didn't know, at the time, the consequences my choice would cause.

Once again, his imagination was drawn to the past. He lost himself in a vague reverie that mingled Iris's joyful face with the dark silhouette presently haunting the Pommier Chenin. Not to mention the words of the "Serenade," which came back to him continually, irritating but beautiful in spite of everything…

Let your breast be moved as mine is,
Darling, hear my cry!
I wait trembling, yearning toward you!
Come, and bring me joy!

Suddenly he heard a muffled thumping: someone was knocking at the door. He flew to open it.

7

PIANO TRIO, OPUS 100

He stood on the doorstep. The wind was prob-
ing the folds of his coat and hanging snowflakes
on his disheveled hair. For an instant, Hermin
thought he was gazing at one of those portraits that show
"the child of the century" in all his poisonous glory, so thoroughly did Lenny's pallor, his pose, his clothing coincide
with a whole lineage of imagery stretching from the German
Romantics to the Pre-Raphaelites they loved. He remained
like that for a few more seconds, unmoving, standing erect
in the open doorway; then he coughed, staggered gradually
forward, slammed the door behind him, and leaned against
it, wheezing and gasping; the spell was broken. Hermin
stepped close to him; he was shivering and struggling to
catch his breath. On his face was a crazed expression the
young composer had never seen there before.

"Lenny...Lenny, are you okay?"

Lenny nodded and laboriously stood upright again. When their eyes met, his dilated pupils fastened on his friend's with a gleam of despair. "Hermin," he said in a muffled voice, turning away to take off his coat. "We have to talk."

Hermin didn't ask what he meant.

One day the concierge in my apartment building hailed me as I was arriving home.

"Monsieur Peyre!" she exclaimed, visibly eager to speak to me. "I was waiting for you...A young man came to see you in the middle of the afternoon—he said it was urgent..."

"A student?" I asked, repressing a sigh. I was vaguely thinking of a boy, an acquaintance, who was supposed to return my harmony textbook along with a copy of Berlioz's Treatise on Orchestration—nothing that qualified, in my opinion, as "urgent."

"He didn't leave his name, but he wanted you to meet him at the Werther..."

This time I sighed aloud. It was raining, I was exhausted, and I most certainly did not feel like going out again.

They went into the Great Room. Lenny pulled one of the armchairs close to the fire and let himself drop onto the upholstered seat. He was still shivering.

"It's starting to snow hard," he murmured, as though justifying himself, before resuming in a different tone: "Can we have a drink?"

The young composer raised his eyebrows and opened the lower door of the sideboard, revealing half a dozen bottles he'd hardly ever had an occasion to open. He read out the names and then added, "If you're cold, I can fix you some mulled wine..."

Lenny declined the offer and chose brandy. Hermin poured two glasses and sat in front of the fireplace, facing the young man. For a moment they remained unmoving, drinking silently. Lenny's face was still pale, but his trembling had calmed down.

"Suppose I put on some music?" Hermin suggested, less out of a real desire to hear something than wishing to break the silence that was about to envelop them.

The youth made a vague head movement without taking his eyes off his glass. Choosing to take this as a sign of assent, the young composer began to search his collection for the piece that could best accompany their evening. For an instant, his hand hesitated over his friend's recordings— Schumann's *Kreisleriana*, Liszt's *Années de pèlerinage*, or better yet, his transcriptions of lieder by Schubert—but then he gave up that idea, anxious to avoid any possibility of disagreement, and in the end he put on Schubert's opus 100 Piano Trio. At the first measures, a smile of approbation played on Lenny's lips. The work was, without a doubt, one of his favorites, and Hermin remembered a period when the boy, who was crazy about the second movement, would cue it up again and again, with hardly a pause, on the player in the garret room. Now that time seemed very far away...But maybe it had never been so close.

However, a suspicion crossed my mind. "Tell me," I said to the concierge, "did he have a foreign accent?"

"Ah, yes..." she said.

She'd been a little girl during the Occupation and had never forgotten the "boches" and their accents...And there I cut her short.

All of a sudden, the young man put down his glass and raised his head. "Do you think I have changed?"

The question, asked so abruptly, made the young composer wince, for it very nearly echoed those that had occupied him since Lenny's reappearance. The opportunity was, perhaps, unique; Hermin would have liked to make a sincere reply.

"I...I believe so, yes. It's hard to say—we've grown older, and I don't know much about how you've lived all this time..."

"I thought about you."

Lenny made this declaration in a toneless voice, as if he wished at all costs to avoid emphasizing the intimate character of his confession; moreover, a delivery so lackluster had the virtue—or the drawback, according to one's point of view—of maintaining a certain ambiguity; did he want to indicate that his lost friend had been his sole thought, or had he simply interrupted Hermin by way of changing the subject? After a moment of uncertainty, the young composer, seeing that Lenny would say no more, chose to go on, without any very clear idea of what to say: "Well, anyway, I have the impression you're not completely the same. I don't know for sure, of course...Maybe it's just an idea..."

"And...how changed?" the young man asked in one breath.

"I'd say that you've calmed down. You would never have stayed so...so passive, if you'll excuse the word...Which is only normal, of course, you're not fifteen anymore...You were...how shall I say it...more passionate, more impulsive, you couldn't be still, you flew into a rage over nothing..."

"Do you miss it?"

This time Hermin would have sworn that Lenny hadn't premeditated the question before blurting it out. "I don't know. Maybe."

"I see..." the young man murmured. A strange gleam lit his eyes. "I thought that was what you couldn't stand..."

He poured himself another glass of brandy.

As I headed for the Werther, I couldn't help thinking that I was scurrying along for nothing. It was after seven o'clock, and I couldn't imagine that the boy would have waited that long for me. But I wasn't sure, so I couldn't shirk our rendezvous. Besides, I wondered about what an "urgent" reason might be...

Already in those days, Lenny tended toward obstinacy. Naturally, I found him standing at the café entrance, sheltered from the rain by a canvas awning, shivering in the moisture-laden air. I didn't make the mistake of asking him why he was waiting outside; I knew he didn't have enough money to pay for a drink.

As they had done on the previous evenings, once again they listened silently to Schubert's Piano Trio No. 2. While the *Andante* was getting under way—the famous C minor *Andante*, rhythmical though slow, the true domain of the Schubertian Wanderer, at once funeral march and song of a lost Paradise, a final journey that would be accompanied in the following year (the composer's last) by the 2/4 tempo of another *Andante*, the *Andante con moto* of the C Major Symphony, known as "the Great"—Hermin recalled one of their projects, which had come to nothing, but which had involved recording that same trio, or at least presenting it in concert, since the piano, the violin, and the cello happened to be the instruments played by, respectively, Lenny, Iris, and himself. They had also considered Chopin's Piano Trio, a veritable chamber concerto for piano in which the boy would have had the leading role. Later, when any sort of concord between him and the girl had grown impossible, Lenny had suggested to Hermin that they two should collaborate on the Arpeggione; they had even begun to work on it, each on his own part... But their separation had put an end to the project. And yet...

As Hermin listened to that poignant, nostalgic work—or so he perceived it at present—he found himself feeling regret for having missed a different life, a life in which he and Lenny, and maybe Iris, would have been able to form an ensemble like the Trio Wanderer, the French piano trio Lenny had always admired, and whose name the young pianist had been jealous of without knowing that he himself was to receive the same sobriquet from a rhapsodic reviewer, who would waste no time in sharing his discovery with the musical world…In point of fact, they were still young enough to set out on such an adventure today, but Lenny's refusal was too predictable for his friend even to think about submitting the idea to him, and that certainty caused him—Hermin—something like obscure resentment. Or like remorse.

"Well, what's going on?" I asked, right off the bat.

Lenny raised his strained face to me, as if he were searching for words, or for the best way to present the situation.

"My aunt is in the hospital," he said. "This morning she cannot breathe…I had the Doktor *come, and after he saw her then he called the ambulance himself…because of her age, he must watch her close…"*

With a knot in my throat, I put my hand on the boy's shoulder in a gesture of compassion. "She'll be all right, Lenny…They're going to take care of her…" My voice was low but firm, even though those words, in the moment when I pronounced them, sounded false.

He shook his head and then turned away.

Now they were observing each other alternately, like cats that scrutinize their adversary while it looks off to one side and then lower their gaze so that the other can stare in its turn; the objective was to know who would break the silence, and to what end. The cello's long-breathed song was still swirling around the room, but for what was doubtless the first time, they had stopped listening to it. Lenny seemed especially distraught and nervous. He drummed his fingers on the mantelpiece, bit his lip like a child, coughed a little. Sometimes he looked to be on the verge of saying something, but then he changed his mind. In quick succession, he emptied his second glass and poured himself a third. The resolve to speak that he'd expressed upon his return seemed to have gone missing; he no longer dared. In itself, this about-face was no surprise to Hermin, for in it he recognized his friend's most consistent character trait: an unhealthy shyness, poorly concealed by counterfeit self-assurance and superficially rebellious words, an assertiveness ready to crumble away should a sensitive subject arise. The fear of being misjudged or held in contempt tormented him incessantly; and even in the young composer's company, he seemed never to have really let his guard down—which was even less likely to happen in a moment like the present one, when they were striving to get out from under the double burden of a painful past and an uncertain future. After a brief hesitation, Hermin wanted to come to the boy's aid.

"How about me? Have I changed?"

Lenny raised his head. Once again, his eyes met his friend's. "No," he murmured in a muffled voice.

Then he was silent for a few seconds before going on, as though throwing himself into deep water: "You know, we must not the past regret. We have to talk…"

Hermin felt that Lenny was close to the crucial point, which maybe it was now possible for them to reach; he wanted to help him. "Listen to me, Lenny," he said. "You were my best friend ten years ago, and whatever you may have done, you still are."

But this declaration was perhaps too grandiloquent, and in any case didn't have the soothing effect Hermin had counted on. At first, a rictus contorted Lenny's mouth. Then, one second later, he was again impassive. The young composer hesitated to interpret the grimace he'd glimpsed; maybe the reflection of the flames had played a trick on him…

"Hermin…" *he began again, his voice muffled.* "Is…is the…" *He broke off.*

"Yes?" *I said to get him started again, as gently as I could. His features were noticeably contorted, and his cheeks had turned crimson, as though he were in the throes of some deep confusion.*

"The hospital…complicated…" *he stammered, pretty incoherently.* "A long way from home…"

I felt a sudden surge of pity, imagining the boy alone, lost in the middle of the city, far from his aunt. He was only sixteen years old... What did he expect from me?

"Thanks," the young man managed to articulate. But the timbre of his voice was muted, almost inaudible.

Making an effort to seem composed, he emptied his glass and grabbed the bottle again. Hermin, stunned by the expression he'd seen cross Lenny's face, bit the inside of his cheek. "If I were you, I'd stop," he said, in a voice he tried his best to keep even.

"And if I were you, I would stop treating me like a kid!" the young man replied, violently setting down the bottle. "You say I have changed, but you look like you think I am still fifteen..."

Surprised by this outburst, Hermin made no answer.

"Lenny, explain yourself clearly for once! I'm not going to eat you..."

He frowned, and I realised, a bit late, that he didn't understand the expression. I tried again: "Come on, you know you can ask me for whatever you want..."

I saw a gleam of hope in his eyes.

"Really?"

"I wouldn't say so otherwise," said I, with a smile—but not without a twinge of disquiet: What could the boy possibly be thinking?

"Well then, can I stay with you?"

With a sigh, Lenny dropped onto the armchair, rummaged around in his still-damp hair, and started talking again, his voice hoarse: "If I told you I am not drunk and you must listen to me, you would not believe, would you?"

"That depends," Hermin replied, almost on the defensive.

He was starting to find the boy's behavior not so much moving as irritating.

"You miss the good old days, is this not right?"

Hermin nodded bitterly. Lenny slumped deeper in the chair.

"Well, if you love the past, it means you did not understand…"

Hermin felt himself seized by sudden anger, no doubt repressed and nourished, unbeknownst to him, ever since their reunion, yet he chose to yield to the feeling without resistance. "If you want to talk, fine, I'm all for it, but explain yourself clearly!"

Lenny took a big breath and tensed his lips, which had up to then been trembling. His wide-open eyes seemed to be staring into an abyss visible only to himself; had he been a child, he would have appeared to be on the brink of tears. Maybe he was getting ready to speak, but Hermin could see only his worried face and his fingers jerking around on his empty glass; then, at the moment when the young man opened his mouth, Hermin cut him off: "Let's stop right here. You're drunk, and for that matter so am I, and night fell a long time ago. We'll have time to pick up this conversation tomorrow."

He got up, stopped the record, even though it was reaching the end—he who had always declared that "stopping one of Schubert's pieces in the middle of a measure was a crime against humanity"—and then turned away.

It was my turn to frown without understanding. He must have misinterpreted my reaction, and he quickly went on: "I will not disturb you, it is my promise! I will leave as soon as when my aunt gets out of the hospital..."

He was asking me to put him up...I'd expected worse. I'd frequently let foreign students I'd met at the Conservatory stay in my garret, and I'd never had cause to regret it. "You'll be welcome," I said without hesitating.

However, as Hermin was preparing to leave the room, a voice stopped him: "Wait!"

Hermin executed a half turn. Lenny too was on his feet, standing before the fireplace and leaning on the hob. A coughing fit interrupted him; he swayed, tried to calm his agitated breathing, moved close to Hermin, and caught him by one arm. "Wait, Hermin. You must promise me one thing at least..."

No doubt, weariness and pique at having failed increased Hermin's anger, but the bad faith it provoked made him attribute his exasperation to the boy's behavior alone, and so he let

Lenny make matters worse: "You have one thing to promise me, no, to swear...to swear that you will not blame me...even if you think I am wrong..."

How could I have guessed at the time that the boy would spend not two days, not even two weeks, but two years in my company?

For an instant, Hermin, more infuriated than surprised by the boy's untoward request, thought about refusing, about demanding explanations, but such a reaction would have prolonged the evening in vain, and the only thing he wanted was rest. The best course was to assent to Lenny's request. By the next day, all would be forgotten...

"I promise..."

While he was thanking me effusively, I was certainly far from imagining that my life would be so completely transformed. And yet, where that boy was concerned, I should already have been prepared for anything.

Lenny closed his eyes and released Hermin's arm. "Thank you."

8

COURAGE!

The thread of days continued to unspool. Storms and calms succeeded one another with the metronomic regularity of the quarrels and reconciliations that had formerly marked the rhythm of the young men's lives. Most of the time, the snow piled up on the threshold and blocked the door so effectively that they couldn't escape each other; Lenny thought about his wanderings, Hermin about his music, and nothing brought them together. Moreover, they almost succeeded in avoiding each other completely, so raw was the memory of their last shared evening. One of them remained in his own room while the other occupied the Great Room, and vice versa. Sometimes, running into each other in the corridors, they would exchange remarks in the style of fellow office workers, and all the time, the boy's coughing disturbed the cello's song, even though the young composer no longer dared allude to the other's indisposition. And so the days followed one another. "It's the winter's fault," Hermin occasionally said to himself—or indeed, "It's Lenny's fault"; but that last was a barely conscious thought.

Lenny came and moved in with me, and very soon I had the impression that we'd always lived under the same roof, so natural did his presence seem. He passed his days at the piano, and I had the greatest difficulty tearing him away from it in the evening—which was nevertheless necessary if we were to avoid complaints from the neighbors. For my part, I was under the spell, and even if he had to spend three hours repeating the same measure, I listened to him carefully while going over the material for my music appreciation class. I also got to know him better and learned how to overcome his obstinate silence; the gratitude he felt toward me seemed to have overpowered the last barriers of his shyness, and he showed himself to be a boy full of life, occasionally exuberant, completely different from the timid teenager I'd first met. The only area of tension was my various friendships. On that subject, his mind closed, he argued, he became aggressive.

As soon as a mild spell allowed it, the young composer left the Pommier Chenin and took refuge in his beloved pavilion. During the course of several afternoons, he tried to make progress on his project, transposing fragments of works so that they would gravitate around the dominant key of D, transcribing this or that theme for the instrumental combination he'd finally decided on—a trio for piano, violin, and cello, no surprise, although he refused to see in his choice a preference guided by the past—and constantly writing, erasing, modulating, losing his footing, finding himself unable to meld two melodies harmoniously, starting over, getting no further, giving up. In short, his *Homage* was going nowhere, not so much because of the difficulties it presented but because of the composer's shortcomings. Hermin almost abandoned the project altogether, but doing so would surely have been anything but harmless; he lived with remorse for having failed in another endeavor in which it would have been much more essential for him to succeed; and so he persisted all the more doggedly in this one.

I would have liked to avoid those quarrels, those disagreements, but I refused to sacrifice everything for the boy's sake. I fled from him to see Iris; Iris likewise covered me with reproaches; and thus I found myself incessantly torn between the two musicians, obliged to placate the delicate feelings of each without ever managing to find the balance point. Life was not much fun.

Hermin was working hard: in addition to his composing, he had to see to the firewood and perform the housekeeping chores. Lenny, for his part, did nothing. He seemed to have given up rambling around the house and spent most of his time sitting in an armchair, apathetic, his eyes staring into space. The young composer suspected him of drinking on the sly out of sheer idleness. That was as good a method as any; whether fast or slow, time would always eventually pass.

Soon Lenny went so far as to try to prevent me from going out: on one particularly cold and rainy fall day, seeing that I was putting on a raincoat, he got up from the piano, went over to the door, and leaned against it to block my passage. I tried to shove him aside; he didn't budge. He looked pale and resolute.

"Now you have to choose."

"Choose?"

"Either we work together, or you and Iris go and waste your time in a café."

"Stop, you're being ridiculous. Let me pass!"

I shoved him harder and succeeded in opening the door. For an instant, we struggled together in silence on the threshold. I was stronger than he was. I went out.

One afternoon, however, the normal course of the day was broken, like an hourglass overturned before the last grains of sand have fallen from the upper bulb. By sheer force, Hermin had dug a trench through the snow and made his way to the pavilion. He'd had the idea of giving his *Homage* a unity not only of tonality but also of tempo, with the end of imparting to the whole an implacable rhythm that the binary-ternary sequence had thus far impeded. The inspiration was felicitous, its execution was not; it was hard to reconcile the 2/4 time of "Courage," his secret anthem, with the 3/8 of "Will-o'-the-Wisp," a song dear to Lenny... And so once again, Hermin had worked for hours to no avail. Outside, snow was falling, not thickly, but hard enough so that the composer needed to wield his shovel again in order to clear the trench leading back to the Pommier Chenin. As he did so, he sang ironically to himself the first verse of the lied he'd just been working on:

If in my face the snow should blow,
I shake the white flakes off me,
And when my heart speaks in my breast,
I sing out loud and lusty.

And so he reached the house, cold, soaked, exhausted, and, all things considered, in an extremely foul mood. From the doorway, he glanced up at the sky. A most violent storm was gathering itself to strike that night. Those heaped, mauve-tinted clouds, covering a sky whose darkened crystal was visible only in a few scattered points, never presaged anything good. And to think he'd put off cutting more firewood! He inwardly cursed himself.

Lenny caught up with me as I went down the stairs and tried to hold on to my coat. I got free of him. Outside, the driving rain stung my face. I turned up the collar of my raincoat.

*At least, I thought, the weather will keep Lenny from follow-
ing me; all he had on was a thin shirt.*

Hermin stepped into the Great Room, which was getting dim in the fading evening light; it didn't occur to him
that Lenny might be there. The fire was dead and the lights
were off, so it took a few seconds for his eyes to adapt to
the semidarkness and a moment more before he saw the
boy, half-sprawled on the sofa with a glass in his hand. The
brandy bottle near him was three-quarters empty. Hermin
didn't know exactly why, but at this sight, the rage that had
been smoldering inside him for days—rage born of all the
struggles with his *Homage*, all the obscure quarrels, all the
silences—blazed into sudden flame. Without going any
farther into the room, he shouted in a voice vibrating with
anger: "Leonard Wieck!"

The boy sat up a little and turned around. "Hermin?"
he said, hesitating slightly.

"Who else, do you suppose?" the young composer
replied, and strode into the room. "Leonard, I leave you
alone one afternoon and you let the fire go out, plus you're
drunk!"

"I pass the time. Hermin, I have nothing else to do…"

"Nothing to do? There's a whole bunch of things to
do around here! Chop wood, knock the snow off it, bring
it inside, tend the fire, and fix a meal, which is what I've
been doing for days…But such things would never occur to

Monsieur Wieck! He doubtless thinks the local elves take care of them! If you'd at least go back to playing the piano, it would be a little more dignified..."

"Hermin, I was not a pianist because it was *dignified*! I was a pianist because I loved it..."

"And drinking when I'm not here, you do that because you love it too?" the young composer replied, half-angry, half-ironic.

Lenny stared at him for a few seconds, his eyes a little bleary, his pupils bright, dilated.

"I did not say that," he murmured softly.

This change in tone briefly disoriented Hermin. After a slight hesitation, he went and sat down beside the young man. In the growing darkness, his features were barely distinguishable. Only a single ray of light fell on his prominent cheekbone, creating a broken line between night and day. Outside, an evening the color of wine lees descended on the horizon. It was still snowing.

Such thinking underestimated the boy's determination. He came out of the building right behind me, indifferent to the rain drenching his hair and streaming down his neck. "Hermin!" he called from the sidewalk while I stepped rapidly away from him. "Hermin!"

Then, seeing that I wasn't slowing down, he ran out into the street and the traffic, nearly got run over, skidded on the slippery pavement, and joined me, already soaking wet.

"Lenny, what pleasure can you find in this...this lethargy?" Hermin finally asked, his tone less cutting than before.

Lenny hung his head, contemplated his hands, and made up his mind to reply, which he did, hoarsely: "None... no pleasure..."

"But still?"

With a slight movement of his head, the young man sank further into the sofa, as though putting an end to the conversation. Hermin felt a wave of anger surging up in him again. He was on the verge of making a violent reply when Lenny forestalled the outburst by lifting his head—his eyes lost, his lips trembling—and murmuring, "You promised... do you remember? You promised not to blame me..."

"Well, I shouldn't have made that promise! Iris was basically right...She said you'd hold me to ridiculous pledges..."

"Shut up. Please. You know we hated each other. You are doing it on purpose, talking about her..."

"On purpose?" Hermin repeated after the young man's voice trailed off.

"On purpose because you know it hurts me," Lenny said in one breath, sounding even hoarser than usual.

Hermin slowly raised his head. If Lenny had been sober, he would never have said such a thing. Had the occasion finally come to make him talk?

"Hermin...Pleass..." he stammered as he drew even with me.

"'Herman,'—zat's ze only word in your mouz!" said I, wickedly imitating his accent. "Leave me alone, will you? I'm late..."

He recoiled as though I'd slapped him. His lips were trembling; he was on the verge of tears. But I didn't feel like continuing our dispute in the middle of the street. More gently, I put a hand on his shoulder. "Go back home," I said in a soft voice. "I swear I won't be long..."

He hung his head, as though in resignation. Without waiting any longer, I walked away from him and entered the café where Iris had said she'd meet me.

"I mentioned Iris because she was right. The only things that bind us together are forced promises."

"That is not true, I did not force you to take me in!"

"You were just a child, you were alone and penniless. I had no choice..."

"So it was for charity?" Lenny asked, his voice almost inaudible.

Hermin noted that he'd turned even paler. "That's not what I meant," the young composer said, trying to make amends, but his anger soon got the better of him. "Oh, what the hell! Yes, that's it, that's what it was! You didn't see anything, you didn't understand anything...Iris loved me, Lenny!"

Our date wasn't very pleasant. I made the bad mistake of explaining to Iris the reason why I was late, and in return I got to hear long recriminations on the subject of Lenny and the great solicitude—excessive solicitude, in her opinion—that I showed in his regard. I managed to distract her for a moment by relating how Nicolas, a cellist friend of ours, had broken a string on his instrument in the middle of a concert, but soon, by way of a remark about duets for strings and piano, she returned to her fixed idea, about which she was nearly as obstinate as the boy. I got angry and left her within an hour.

The young composer was expecting to see Lenny's face crumple, but to his great surprise, his companion didn't blink an eye. "I knew that," he said dully. "I knew it... The question is, did you love her?"

"You knew?" Hermin replied, carefully avoiding Lenny's question.

"Do not make me explain."

Hermin was on to something. The point Lenny refused to talk about was necessarily the most sensitive point. It was up to him, Hermin, to uncover it. But the young man, oddly distraught, remained mute.

Outside, the rain was still coming down hard. The streets were deserted. Completely deserted? No. Leaning against a wall near the café, alone, shivering, Lenny was waiting for me. When he spotted me, a pale smile lightened his face. He stood up straight, coughed a little, wobbled.

"You're crazy," I told him, but I no longer felt any anger toward him—only pity, not to say affection. "You've been out here in the rain all this time?"

He nodded.

There was a silence. Through the window, Hermin could see the tops of the larches writhing wildly, their branches furiously whipping the glass panes. The twilight still wrested the occasional gleam from the table, the mirror over the fireplace, the candlesticks, but the night was closing in. The night: the *mala noche* of Goya and Gracq, he thought...

"Why not?"

Lenny gnawed his lip. Now he was looking at Hermin like a hunted animal. "Because you will hate me a lot," Lenny said in a broken murmur.

"Not to worry, that's been taken care of already," the young composer, deliberately provocative, assured him.

The effect was immediate. Lenny's face turned the color of ash. He thrust out a hand toward his glass, seemed to catch himself, and left the movement unfinished. "All right, then," he said in a hurried voice, as if he wanted to get the words out and over with. "I know because I read a letter from her."

Hermin stood up. Lenny drew his head down between his hunched shoulders.

"It was addressed to you," he murmured, as if he'd lost all hope of escaping his fate.

It took several seconds for Hermin to realize the full significance of what the boy had just confessed. Then, in a voice distorted by rage: "You read a letter to me from Iris, a love letter, and you didn't give it to me?"

Lenny shut his eyes briefly and nodded. "It was after your last quarrel. She wrote. I found the letter...and sent it back to her."

That affirmation, that pathetic smile, the girl's acrimony— did they get the better of me? I looked at him in silence. Then I heard myself say, "I've made my choice, I'll work with you."

The room had begun to spin. "You did that," Hermin said in a toneless voice.

The boy didn't reply; all replying was useless. Outside the snow was coming down twice as thick. They were alone now, alone in the house the snowflakes would soon bury, alone with that confession.

"You did that, and you kept on living peacefully under my roof!"

"Not peacefully!" Lenny, newly energetic, shot back. "Why do you think I left you for?"

"Apparently it didn't stop you from coming back ten years later!" Hermin snapped. Then, beside himself with rage, he went on: "I've been feeding you for a month...It has never occurred to you that it's already hard for me, just by myself, to make it through the winter on what I earn in the summer...Don't get the idea I can keep this up much longer..."

"Feeding you" was an assuredly ignoble assertion, given that the boy was visibly wasting away from day to day. Hermin rejected this thought.

"So you want me to leave?"

"I didn't say that."

"You think that, it is the same."

Hermin hesitated for a fraction of a second, his forehead pressed against the window, but it was too late. "All right. You can leave."

Lenny raised his head, looking incredulous. Our eyes met; he saw my sincerity, and a smile, a happy child's smile, spread slowly over his face.

Outside everything was engulfed in night, the wind blowing harder than ever through the branches, and thousands upon thousands of snowflakes drifting back up into an arctic sky. The storm was starting to break loose.

"Thanks" was all he said.

Hermin turned around; the young man was already on his feet. He swayed a little, leaned on the sofa, and headed for the door. "So long, Hermin," he said.

I patted his shoulder and, arm in arm, running through the rain, we hurried back to the garret.

A moment later, he was gone.

9

DEATH AND THE YOUTH

Immediately, a wave of anguish and remorse swept over Hermin, like the windy blasts that were assaulting the building in distress. He ran to the door, snatched it open, and called out from the threshold: "Lenny! Don't be an idiot! Lenny!"

For all response, some snowflakes, avenging soldiers, stung his face and infiltrated his collar: just punishment for a man who had thrown his guest out on such a hellish night...

At first, a bit of disingenuousness saved him. He imagined that it wouldn't be long before the storm would discourage the boy and oblige him to seek shelter and wait for a lull; soon he'd be knocking on the door...

Hermin went back to the Great Room and numbly took refuge next to the hearth. There the roar of the windy gusts as they rushed furiously down the chimney mingled with raised voices from the scene he'd just lived through to fill the room with sound. Outside the storm was besieging the Pommier Chenin as never before. The windowpanes vibrated under the cannonade.

Now Hermin was trembling. Was that caused by the cold insinuating itself into the house, or was it a repercussion of the recent disaster? His gaze fell on the bottle and the glass that were still standing on the low table. He contemplated them with disgust for several moments, but then, as his shivering persisted, he finally poured himself a shot and downed it in one gulp. After that he fell back into the armchair, trying to remain insensible to the remorse that was beginning to torment him. He saw a book Lenny had left lying open on one arm of the sofa. The work in question—nothing less than a rare edition of Schubert's correspondence—was part of Hermin's music library. He'd perused the volume numerous times and liked reading it piecemeal. It was natural for him, this time, to begin reading at the page where Lenny must have left off. And thus he stumbled on the following passage, in the margin of which a couple of lines of verse had been written in pencil:

Imagine a man who will never be healthy again,
and who out of despair over this constantly makes
things worse instead of better; imagine a man, I

say, whose brightest hopes have turned to naught,
to whom the joys of love and friendship offer
nothing but torment, whose enthusiasm for beauty
threatens to vanish, and ask yourself, is this not a
miserable, unhappy man?

"Yes, he is," said Hermin to himself.

Then, not without difficulty, he deciphered the two
handwritten lines in the margin, recognizing them as verses
from the text of Brahms's *Alto Rhapsody*:

Ach, wer heilet die Schmerzen
*Des, dem Balsam zu Gift ward?**

Of course, he wasn't the one who'd written those lines.

I must reiterate that after the first weeks of our cohab-
itation had passed, our relationship began to deteriorate.
Lenny seemed to be devoured by spite, made scenes when I
went out to spend time with others—in his mind, "others"
meant Iris—and stopped me from leaving the garret when-
ever he could. I reacted by treating him with a degree of irri-
tability and rudeness that was doubtless excessive. It wasn't
only our music that our neighbors complained about, but also
our loud, incessant rows—and our neighbors, I admit, were

---

* "Ah, who can soothe the pain he feels / Whose balm has turned to poison?" (Goethe, *Harzreise im Winter*).

right. One thing was sure: at that rate, we wouldn't go on living together for long.

Schubert's letter was dated March 3, 1824, and therefore more or less contemporaneous with the period when he was writing his "Death and the Maiden" string quartet. Poor Franz was twenty-seven years old at the time—the same age as Lenny, according to Hermin's rapid calculation. Could the boy have found that the letter cast an interesting light on the mournful variations of the second movement? Something like that, no doubt... It was best to stick to musicological considerations—and try to forget the fleeting grimace that had distorted Lenny's features a few days earlier when Hermin declared, "You're still my best friend."

"A man to whom the joys of love and friendship offer nothing but torment..."

Hermin snapped the book shut. He'd bought it used, after all. Maybe its previous owner had annotated it, and Lenny had had nothing to do with writing those lines in the margin...

Lenny...

No. Don't think about that.

It was in those days when I finally met his aunt, who remained in the hospital. I was a little fearful, I admit it, about that first encounter, without any clear notion why. Maybe I was afraid that paying a visit to a woman I didn't know might be indiscreet, or maybe I feared causing Lenny some embarrassment. In any case, as it turned out, my fears were unfounded. First of all, I was surprised to find myself facing a woman of my grandmother's age—very thin, her skin blanched by the years, her appearance so fragile that a breath would have sufficed to sweep her away. She looked at me quizzically and then asked Lenny a question in German. There followed a brief discussion, of which I understood not a word. At last, she held out one slightly trembling hand to me and introduced herself as Constance.

However, he *did* think about it. Furious at the boy, furious at himself, Hermin poked the fire with hard, forceful thrusts before dropping back into the chair and refilling his glass.

Then he yawned. Sure, it was still early, but he'd had a trying day. He started dreaming about the moment when he would burrow under a pile of bedcovers—and he immediately had the impression that he'd been struck in the center of his chest, like the character in *Les Enfants Terribles* who's hit by a snowball. But which of them, he or Lenny, was Dargelos? That night wouldn't be, couldn't be, anything like those winter nights when he went to bed with peace in his heart, enjoying the warmth of his room in the midst of the ambient cold. A man was wandering in a snowstorm, and it was his, Hermin's, fault!

Constance's French was only rudimentary—more often than not, Lenny served as interpreter when she and I spoke together—but I was surprised to hear that French literary words and somewhat old-fashioned French turns of phrase formed a regular part of her conversation. When I yielded to curiosity and asked her where she'd gotten them from, she answered that she'd often heard her sister sing French art songs. And so her language exhibited a curious intermingling of Paul Verlaine and Pierre Louÿs. Although I found this explanation utterly logical, I was still surprised that she knew Fauré's and Debussy's music so well. Lenny had led me to believe that he'd never studied music at home... When I asked him about this, his face darkened. "My aunt made music, but that was before she starts to take care of me."

He wished to say no more on the subject. Something in his attitude dissuaded me from questioning Constance any further. Quite obviously, there were family secrets I was supposed to stay clear of.

He emptied his glass and then stood up. Now he knew he couldn't spend any more time dithering.

At some point, various snatches of their quarrel had begun colliding with one another in his head again, like sound fragments from a broken record:

"You promised...do you remember? You promised not to blame me..."

"You're doing it on purpose, talking about her..."

"Not peacefully! Why do you think I left you for?"

The stream of words suddenly crystallized.

"Why do you think I left you for?"

A few hours earlier, overcome by rage, Hermin hadn't paid any particular attention to that question, which was nevertheless essential; he saw that now, and he was struck with amazement. He who had not, for ten long years, ever stopped wondering why his friend had vanished so abruptly and so completely, he who had faulted himself in every possible way, convinced that his own behavior had pushed Lenny into leaving—even though he'd never been able to see exactly what he'd done that had been so reprehensible— he now knew the real reason for his friend's flight! The muffled disquiet that had been eating at the boy since his arrival was, therefore, the product of remorse...A new light suddenly illuminated a whole mass of events: the young man's embarrassment several nights earlier when he'd tried, without success, to confess his guilty secret; his grimace at the words "You're still my best friend"; and, above all, his silence, and the promise he'd extracted from Hermin not to blame him...

Hermin now saw that Lenny's remorse had more than sufficiently expiated his adolescent misdeed. Perhaps, without really believing he would receive absolution as a result of his confession, the young man had counted on being absolved, finally relieved of the burden of his fault, of a "sin" that could well be qualified as "original," because— although Hermin knew nothing of it—it had been at the very origin of the breakdown in their friendship. But Lenny had come up against the young composer's anger and had felt obliged to leave, abandoning all hope of redemption...

When the boy had gone away ten years earlier, he'd doubtless thought he was making up for his sin. It would have been so simple for Hermin, once his friend was gone, to explain himself to Iris and take up with her again. Now, Hermin was convinced that Lenny would never have dared to make a reappearance without first learning from a mutual acquaintance—Hermin's friend Philippe Hersant, perhaps, a fellow composer who shared his love for *Winterreise*, or maybe the cellist Nicolas Fiodorov, he of the broken string—that his friend still lived alone, and that he had even withdrawn from Parisian life, opting for what was practically a hermit's existence in the Bourbonnais Mountains. That was when Lenny had decided to join him.

There was, however, one point that remained hard for Hermin to explain: Why had the boy decided to give up the piano? Was it a sort of self-flagellation, or had his decision been totally independent of the "Iris affair"? That question would be best put to the young man himself...

At the same moment, Hermin took a hard look at the assumptions underlying that last reflection. The fever of deduction he'd been gripped by subsided, and he found himself alone in the middle of the Great Room, still trembling, breathing hard. His rancor had dissipated. Now he was thinking about poetic justice: for ten years, Lenny had been tormented by remorse. Would he, Hermin, have to spend the rest of his days bearing up under an equally great remorse, ruing the day when he'd driven out his friend, abandoned him to the fury of the elements, and irremediably ended a friendship that despite everything was his most precious possession? No, of course not. *I'd rather die,* he thought, with the rather ludicrous solemnity that sometimes characterized him.

He'd made his decision. He glanced out the window at the fir trees bending in the wind and shivered again. To boost his courage, he swallowed a last gulp of brandy before equipping himself with a storm lantern. Then he gathered together his winter coat, gloves, scarf, and hat. As he did so, he spotted Lenny's topcoat, still hanging from a hook in the hallway. Hermin froze. Could the boy really have left the house without bothering to put that coat on?

I was equally troubled by a number of traits the two exiles shared in common. I detected in them the same fissure, the same way of withdrawing into a sorrow I knew nothing of. The old woman seemed to be undermined by memories that occasionally lit her black eyes with a distraught glimmer. All things considered, this was not, unfortunately, so very surprising: having lived through the twentieth century in Germany, she'd known the worst. Her memory was most likely filled with terrible images...

The violence of the storm confronted him head-on. In spite of his heavy clothes, he felt the cold seize him by the throat. Was he going to wind up like one of those wretches whom the cruel queen changed into ice for having dared to defy her? Evidently, the only way to escape the curse was to walk, to walk and walk some more, until he found the person who seemed doomed to suffer a worse fate than his...He gave some furtive thought to a few lines from *Winterreise*:

> *Icy gusts lashed at my face;*
> *The cold winds, they were blowing.*
> *My hat went flying off my head,*
> *But I just kept on going...*

Hunching his shoulders in a useless reflex meant to protect him from the cold, he plunged out onto the path, shocked by the absurdity of his own agitation. It had already been an hour since Lenny had taken off into the night... Hermin hesitated, on the point of giving up: Lenny had no doubt found some shelter...But finding him was almost less important to Hermin than searching for him. Hermin must, above all, prove to himself that he was ready to endure the tempest in order to make up for what he'd done and to be able to say, later, that he'd at least tried to help his friend. His eyes fixed on the ground, he thought about the sixth of Debussy's Preludes, "Des pas sur la neige," "Footprints in the Snow." Alas! Within a second, the wind was erasing every step.

That was when he remembered Lenny's nickname. Who was "the Wanderer," if not the man who rambles around aimlessly and for whom the act of walking constitutes an end in itself? Maybe he should just emulate Lenny, Hermin thought, and dash off without a plan in his head...

At the same time, Hermin was well aware that with each passing second, his procrastination was putting more and more distance between him and the boy—if the latter was still wandering around the countryside. Without hesitating any longer, Hermin set out on the road to Arfeuilles.

And so, on the day when I happened to drop the name of Alban Berg—because, simultaneously with the tonal system, I wanted to introduce Lenny to dodecaphony, twelve-tone technique, and I'd recently had him read through some of Berg's pieces for the first time—I saw Constance turn pale, as if I'd awakened an ancient torment. But I told myself that I had doubtless been victimized by my own imagination. After all, she'd lived under a regime in which atonal composers had long been forbidden to work because of their "bourgeois elitism." Maybe the simple explanation was that old prejudices were regaining the upper hand...

The road was already disappearing, and the halo shed by his lamp extended no more than a few paces, with the result that he stumbled incessantly. A fir branch unloaded its snowy burden as he passed underneath it; he felt a gelid mass land on his head and shoulders and run down the length of his spine. He began to shiver convulsively, stopped walking, and to give himself courage repeated the same stanza as before; then he sustained his effort by reciting entire passages from *Winterreise*. After a while, he started calling out Lenny's name—a pure waste of breath, as he well knew. He resumed his march.

What was certain was that her memories' secret sorrows increased her physical weakness. It didn't take long for me to realize that Constance was suffering from a lung disease— whether tuberculosis or cancer, I couldn't say. She breathed with difficulty and was regularly overwhelmed by harrowing coughing fits that sometimes made her spit blood. At such moments, Lenny and I were weighed down with a feeling of helplessness as oppressive as the hostile cough that cut off her respiration. The boy clenched his fists hard enough to hurt himself and rushed to her bedside without being able to help her in any way. I felt his fear, as well as his rage, and I didn't know what to say. Constance looked doomed to me; her state filled me with the greatest sorrow, for she was as lovable as her adopted son—to say nothing of the heartbreak her loss would cause him.

Before long, he became certain that the young man couldn't have resisted the cold for very long, dressed as he was in a simple wool sweater, and that thought chilled Hermin more than he'd been chilled by the snow down his back. He came to a halt in the very middle of the road, unsure what to do, and called again. His cry dwindled away. Then, increasingly desperate, his mind confused and distraught, Hermin started to run almost haphazardly—this too, perhaps, the effect of the alcohol. Fragments of *Winterreise* blew through his head like gusts of wind:

> *The soles of both my feet are burning,*
> *Although I tread on ice and snow...*

> *It was too cold for standing still...*

> *A charcoal-burner's tiny shack*
> *Was all the refuge that I found...*

Of course! Now he knew where the boy was.

Hermin made an abrupt about-face and began to run in the direction of the Pommier Chenin. This time the wind was blowing from behind him, which simplified his task, but he couldn't stop himself from casting a glance at the foliage madly twisting and writhing on his left, at the edge of the woods. By daylight, he could have plunged directly into the forest and thus saved precious time, but on this wild night, even thinking about doing so was out of the question. And so he had to retrace his steps all the way back to his starting point, namely the courtyard of the Pommier Chenin. Then he struck out toward the steep path that led up to the little wood—the same path he'd nearly killed himself clearing that very afternoon. The latest precipitations had practically wiped out his labor, but the snow still looked packed down, as if someone had passed over it a few seconds earlier. So he'd guessed right...

Fighting hand-to-hand with the branches that whipped his face, cursing the snow that impeded his progress, he arrived at the top of the path and dove into the woods without stopping to catch his breath.

"A charcoal-burner's tiny shack..."

At last he reached the music pavilion. No lights. Could he have made a mistake?

After some time had passed, the hospital staff decided to send her to a center in the Paris region, a sort of sanatorium. The departure was painful. Would we ever see her again? For Lenny it was, after the hospitalization that had separated them in the first place, a second upheaval. For several days, he walled himself up in a silence from which I was unable to distract him. Not long afterward, he fell sick. His

bronchitis turned into pneumonia, and for a month he was in
a very bad way. I took care of him day and night, even going
so far as to miss classes for his sake. His feverish gaze, his
frightened child's demeanor pursued me wherever I was and
gave me no rest.

The light from his storm lantern swept over the book-
shelves and the worktable and came to rest on the trembling
body lying half under it. Hermin rushed to his friend's side.
"Lenny," he murmured in a faltering voice.

The boy looked nearly unconscious, but when he heard
his name, he moved his head a little and slightly opened
his eyelids. His feverish eyes met Hermin's. Lenny tried
to speak; a coughing fit carried off his words. Without
waiting any longer, the young composer straightened up
and set about making a fire. The kindling was damp. He
wasted a box of matches before he could coax forth a flame
robust enough to ignite the logs. A few feet away, Lenny was
shaken by another round of coughing. Hermin wielded the
bellows at length, determined to produce a blaze the devil
himself would be jealous of. It was vitally important that the
boy should warm up, and to warm him up, they needed a
fire as hot as a blacksmith's forge. For his part, Hermin was
overheated; his efforts had soaked him in perspiration. He
seized the boy under the arms and dragged him to a spot
in front of the fireplace. He'd hoped that Lenny would stop

shaking once he came into contact with the warm air, but nothing of the sort happened. His irresolution now augmented by panic, Hermin contemplated his friend for a moment; the suffering that altered his features, far from disfiguring him, seemed to increase his beauty. Behind his half-closed lids, his eyes were bright with tears. A wave of emotion broke over the young composer. It was no longer the twenty-seven-year-old Lenny lying there at his feet, but the vulnerable teenager Hermin had looked after a decade before. He felt a cramp in his heart. His present task was to communicate his own warmth to his friend's body, which was getting colder; and although normally he would have hesitated to put his hand even on Lenny's shoulder, now he started hastily pulling off the youth's sweater and shirt. He was appalled by the protruding ribs, and with a kind of rage, he began to rub Lenny down. It was a question of reviving nothing less than the flickering flame of a life...

Lenny, I must admit, was an angelic patient. He never complained, stoically swallowed his prescribed medications, and contented himself with listening to me play the cello or, when his fever was too high or his cough too unbearable, with murmuring my name and gazing at me glassy-eyed. Dare I confess it? That month of illness was, so to speak, the apotheosis of our friendship: for never, I believe, did I feel the bonds that united us more strongly than in those moments.

Lenny rolled his head over to one side. Once again, his eyes met Hermin's. He mumbled some incoherent words—something like *"So kalt...einsam...wie der Schnee..."**

His eyes fixed on Lenny's lips, which were still trembling and occasionally twisted into a grimace of pain, Hermin redoubled his efforts. He'd ceased all thought, knowing instinctively that the frenzy inhabiting him was the only way to save Lenny's life, and that he must not weaken, not at any cost. When he rubbed too vigorously, the boy's jaw clenched; but Hermin persisted, crimson-cheeked, insensible to the battering the pavilion was taking. At that instant, the world was reduced to nothing but what his field of vision encompassed: a corner of the fireplace, glowing embers, a rug with a complicated design, and a shuddering human chest. The rest no longer existed.

Nonetheless, the moment came when all his breath was gone, and he had to stop. He straightened up a little. Realizing his shirt was drenched, he took it off and gazed at Lenny, who had closed his eyes. Then Hermin pulled a blanket over the youth, lay down beside him, and took him in his arms.

---

* "So cold...lonely...like the snow..."

10

REST

It was the cold that, sometime later, woke them up. Hermin, curled into a ball, was shivering convulsively. Despite the headache pounding at his temples, he half opened his eyes. A pale morning granted the still-sleeping pavilion a few rays of that grayish, bluish, almost nacreous light that lends a characteristic shade to winter dawns; it must be early. Cautiously, he turned his head toward the hearth; the fire was out, and the ashes weren't even glowing anymore. No wonder he was freezing to death...Lenny had opened his eyes and was looking at Hermin through bright, feverish, dilated pupils. He was shivering too. His swollen lips bore a hint of a smile. He muttered a few inaudible words and then repeated, "Hermin...Hermin..." before a coughing fit interrupted him. They'd moved in their sleep, but his burning hand was still clutching his friend's icy one.

Eventually he got well, but the illness left him broken, enervated, just barely capable, after a week of convalescence, to take a few steps in the garret room and hold a brief conversation—brief, because every word, every sentence, I observed, required of him not only an effort to articulate the words, but also and above all intense concentration in order to disentangle his French from his German. As for the piano, it was out of the question—and all the more so because I knew his propensity for wearing himself out at the keyboard, sometimes playing for eight consecutive hours before suddenly falling onto his bed, his strength at an end, his day over.

Hermin stood up brusquely, unable to withstand the boy's gaze any longer. He felt troubled, and his disquiet doubtless had more to do with his hallucinatory memory of the previous evening than with their argument. Hermin turned away, refusing to see the pained look that had come over Lenny's face when he'd withdrawn his hand. Noticing his shirt lying abandoned near the table, Hermin slipped it on and then went back to the fireplace to revive the fire. Eventually, figuring he could no longer ignore the presence of the sick person with him, he knelt down beside Lenny and asked, "How do you feel?"

"*Ich weiß es nicht…mir tut der Hals weh…ich denke, ich habe Fieber…aber es ist nicht ernst…*" the young man replied hoarsely, making a vain attempt to smile.

For once, Hermin didn't need a translation; eleven years earlier, he'd heard the same words repeated from time to time by Constance, on the verge of death but determined to reassure them.

In spite of everything, this was a happy period; our quarrels had ceased, and the days and nights when I nursed him without stint had done more to strengthen the bond between us than any other event could have done. Every evening, I was in a hurry to leave the Conservatory, and he would welcome me home joyously. As soon as he was capable of giving me his attention at greater length, I undertook to perfect his musical knowledge.

Nevertheless, the boy must have realized his linguistic confusion, for he corrected himself: "I meant to say...I have a sore throat...and maybe a fever...I do not know...But it is not serious..."

He closed his eyes, as though those few words had worn him out.

"Good. Do you think you can make it back to the Pommier Chenin?" asked Hermin, in a voice that was supposed to sound resolute.

Lonny tried to get up; a violent coughing fit prevented him. He groped for his friend's arm, seized it, immediately began to totter, and collapsed rather than sat on the office chair. Hermin considered him a moment, looked around for the clothes he'd stripped off him the night before, and gathered them up. "Can you put these back on? Wait for me, I'll be right back...I'm going to get you settled in here..."

He opened the door of the pavilion. A layer of ice imprisoned the surroundings like the quartz chunks you find in the mountains, perfectly white, softly glittering, and which, once they're broken, reveal nothing but a fragment of dark rock. During the night, he thought, he and Lenny had constituted, in the heart of a remote landscape, that hard and burning core.

In fact, for a year we'd been mostly focused on developing his technique and his sensibility. Now, as I discovered, his acquaintance with music history was, at best, full of gaps; basically, he knew only those works that were part of his repertoire or my own—which, I admit, came down (for the most part) to Schubert, Schumann, Brahms, and Mahler, my composers of choice. I bought a whole series of cassettes for him to listen to in my absence and gave him scores to read. Every evening, I introduced him to a composer and his most remarkable works; Lenny asked a lot of questions that obliged us to turn to encyclopedias, and that was how we provided ourselves with a solid historical education.

Hermin sank in snow up to his knees as he went back down to the Pommier Chenin, but that was, for a change, the least of his worries. Once inside, he gathered together a light mattress, three warm blankets, and two pillows. Then he took the time to breathe a little.

What had happened, exactly? What was there for him to feel guilty about? He'd always believed, deep down inside, that he was a reasonable, prudent, sometimes even fainthearted man, and he'd upbraid himself on the occasions when he'd been unable to mount a vigorous defense of one of his compositions in the face of criticism—in fact, he had a strong feeling that he wasn't fit to struggle against adversity. He groaned and clapped his hands to his temples, now burning hot. His thoughts wandered a moment—and then, suddenly, this question: What had he felt when he'd snatched the boy's shirt off, when he'd struggled to counteract the fever that was taking hold of him, when he'd finally embraced him to stave off the cold? He knew, but the emotion had been as violent as it was unexpected, and he dared not name it. To do so would have definitively fixed what could still remain unformulated, would have kept alive a memory that asked only to sink into limbo. And so he stopped himself, as though before a door, slightly ajar, that he had no wish to open further. Nonetheless, he couldn't suppress another question: Assuming Lenny had been conscious at that moment, what could he have felt, what could he have imagined? Hermin saw himself as a tightrope walker, precariously balanced above the void...

However, there was an aspect of our companionship that tormented me and that I never mentioned to Lenny: trivial as it may seem, it had to do with money. Up until then, I'd

managed to make ends meet by working part-time at the music
store. The boy's arrival hadn't made my task any easier, and
his illness had finished the process of emptying my wallet.
Moreover, as I thought about the future, I became aware of
the necessity of enrolling Lenny in the Conservatory—I had
no doubt that he'd easily pass the entrance examination—
without any assurance that he'd be able to get a scholarship.
What were we going to do?

When Hermin got back to the pavilion, Lenny was dozing, but upon hearing his friend he opened his eyes and sat
up. Without a word, he watched Hermin prepare the make-
shift bed and then cover him up in a warm woolen blanket.
Involuntarily, the young composer found himself repeating
the same movements that had been familiar to him ten years
previously, and he pressed his lips together to prevent the
same soothing words from exiting his mouth. Almost unbeknownst to him, a fierce struggle was being waged between
the excessive solicitude, the anxiety he was tempted to put
on display, and his determination to keep all emotion at a
distance: the tightrope, once again…

"Is that better?" he asked when he'd finished.

The young man didn't answer right away. He turned a
pensive gaze on his friend and then lost himself for a moment
in the contemplation of the frost whose crystalline arabesques
adorned the windowpanes. Hermin had to prick up his ears
to catch the few words that Lenny finally murmured:

Nun merk' ich erst, wie müd' ich bin,
Da ich zur Ruh' mich lege…

"I only feel how tired I am
Now, when I lay me down…"

The song the lines were from—"Rest," from *Winterreise*—was one of those that Hermin himself had evoked the previous evening while looking for Lenny… The boy had indeed found refuge in the equivalent of "a charcoal-burner's tiny shack"; but Hermin wasn't sure he understood what Lenny meant by citing those two lines.

The solution, however—once I decided to consider it— was simple: I would have to work not just a few mornings a week, but every single day, to augment my income and allow the boy to enroll in the Conservatory. This would also mean I'd have to withdraw from some of my courses, for example orchestral conducting   I surely wasn't going to forsake composition—and bringing myself to do that was hard; but I had no choice.

"Listen," Hermin said after a while, "we're going to wait a little…As soon as the roads have been cleared of snow, I'll take you to the doctor in Renaison…"

The boy signaled his assent with a feeble gesture. Hermin, who had feared a refusal, felt the weight on his shoulders diminish a bit. He was going to sit at his desk when

Lenny seized his arm—or better, tried to seize it, but succeeded only in grazing it with powerless fingers. "No..." he said. "Stay here... *neben mir...*"*

It crossed Hermin's mind that he should flee the pavilion and escape those needy eyes, but he thought better of the idea. Can you refuse a sick person's demands, especially when it's so easy to satisfy them?

Hermin sighed and sat on the floor, his back against the mantelpiece. An indeterminate amount of time passed like that in the silent room. Lenny seemed to have fallen asleep again, but his body was shaken by long tremors; now and then he coughed. As for Hermin, in spite of his throbbing headache, he sank into an agitated somnolence; it was a thought—at first barely formed, then as violent as breaking glass—that yanked him out of his semiconscious state.

But the hardest thing, obviously, was informing the boy of my plans. One morning when he was napping on the sofa while I made breakfast, I tried to explain my reasoning to him— clumsily, no doubt—avoiding his gaze as I did so. He remained silent awhile, long enough for me to ask him if he'd heard me. Our eyes met. His were black, and his lips were trembling.

Had the boy tried to take his own life? Yes or no? The previous evening, he'd run out into the snowstorm without bothering to put on heavy clothes. Having taken refuge in

---

* "Next to me..."

the pavilion, he hadn't tried to make a fire to warm himself. If he, Hermin, had stayed inside, would he now have Lenny's death on his conscience? That would be just like Lenny, finding a clever way to haunt him to the very end and beyond! Hermin immediately took back that mean thought. No, if the young man had acted like that, it was out of despair, and that despair was of Hermin's making. He hadn't tried to understand his reasons, he'd reproached him too much, too harshly, and he'd driven him out without a word. But was that enough? Once again, he remembered Schubert's letter; if it was indeed Lenny who'd made those marginal notes, then his torments had begun before their dispute... Which didn't mean that Hermin was completely absolved of guilt: the boy had been his guest for several weeks; he should have paid more attention to what was gnawing at his young friend's heart, should have tried to get to the bottom of things...Perhaps it wasn't too late, but would he have the nerve? Because, if he was in one way or another responsible for the young man's state—and after all, nothing excluded the possibility that he was innocent of Lenny's malaise—would he be able to bear hearing the truth?

"Why did you not say anything?" he finally asked, getting ready to rebel.

"You had bigger fish to fry."

Lenny frowned—the expression no doubt seemed obscure to him—but he went on, his voice sounding more and more *incensed: "I would have known, I would have done some-thing. I am sixteen, I can work too...And beside, I do not care about entering Conservatory, I want to make piano with you, that is all!"*

"Don't be an idiot, you know very well it's obligatory!"

But he kept talking as if I hadn't said anything. "And beside, if you work every day, we never see each other anymore!"

Hermin's reflections had reached this point when he stopped and sneezed several times.

"Hermin?" said the youth uncertainly. "If you're cold, come get under the covers..."

At one time or another in former days, they had happened to take refuge in the same bed to sleep, but after the night they'd just spent together, Lenny's proposal left Hermin almost without a response. "I'm not cold," he said.

"But...if you want..."

"I'm fine," Hermin said, a little too curtly.

The boy hung his head.

"Stop being so dramatic, we'll see each other every evening!"

He sniggered. "Right, one hour of the whole day!"

"I don't have a choice."

"You have always an excuse! Before Iris, now this..."

I raised my eyes skyward in exasperation. There was always a moment in our arguments when the girl's name was brought up, and I found those moments supremely offensive. I let him know this. He fell silent an instant, and then: "If you do it, I quit the piano!"

Of course, Lenny probably didn't have any very clear memory of the previous evening. All he knew was that they had spent the night in each other's arms…

I gave him a mocking look. "You should have said so before! If you want to give up music, well then—"

"I did not say that," he interrupted me, his voice suddenly fragile.

He was trembling a little, as though our energetic exchange had tired him out. I helped him get back to the sofa and sat down beside him.

Hermin shot the boy a furtive glance. His clenched hands, his rounded back suddenly evoked another silhouette. "Constance…" Hermin said, as though to himself. "You're like her."

Lenny raised his head and smiled slightly. "A nice way to tell me I'll be dead soon."

Hermin's heart skipped a beat. "Don't interpret everything the wrong way! It's just…your attitude, how your mind works…"

"Not more reassuring, I don't think."

Of course not, the young composer thought. Constance's disease had killed her, but not by itself; her wounds had been equally responsible, eating away at her little by little, maybe for years and years, depriving her of all rest, of all hope—but as for finding out what had caused those wounds…

If he unlocked the old woman's secret, would he unlock his friend's at the same time? In former days, he hadn't dared ask questions. Ten years later, couldn't he assume that the statute of limitations had expired? "Lenny…" he began again, hovering between fear and audacity, "you've never told me why you and your aunt left Germany…"

The boy turned his eyes away from the frost-covered window. "Really? It is a complicated story…"

"Listen," I said, speaking more gently, "if you have a better idea, tell me what it is…I've thought about this for a long time."

"You can borrow some money…"

Already Hermin was sorry he'd asked. To extract a lengthy narrative from the young man was hardly the shrewdest way of proceeding…However, Lenny set about answering the question: "My aunt had a son, since a long time disappeared. Alban. People let her think he left the country to become concert artist…One day she found out about his political actions and his arrest, but she always kept hope…As soon as she could leave Berlin, she wanted to go to Paris and try to find his trail."

"And?"

"Nothing, of course. But right to the end, she always kept up hope, like this..." Lenny smiled a gloomy smile. "In fact," he went on, "you are right to say I am like her..."

Hermin declined to pursue this line, returning to a point that had bothered him: "He wanted to be a 'concert artist,' you said? So there were musicians in your family?"

"My aunt was piano teacher. But after her son disappeared, she did not want to play anymore...The whole time I was a child, I was seeing the instrument in the living room, but not allowed to touch it, so I improvise in secret...I dreamed about that..."

The image of the solitary boy who'd appeared in the store one fall afternoon had never stopped intriguing Hermin. How could the young man have got up the nerve to come through the door and improvise so resolutely on an unfamiliar instrument? Now Hermin had the answer...

"From whom?"

"I do not know. Iris..."

"She's as broke as we are!"

"Not her parents."

"I don't know them."

"Yes, but maybe if she is not angry with them anymore "

Another question immediately arose: If Constance had given up the piano after her son's disappearance, should Hermin suppose some similar incident in Lenny's case?

Maybe he too had lost someone dear to him—someone without whom playing music wasn't worth the trouble…

"Lenny," he began, "has there been—"

He broke off. No, if his hypothesis was correct, this wasn't the proper moment to reawaken the boy's grief…

"Yes?"

I was getting ready to tell him how unrealistic his solution to our problem was when I encountered his beseeching gaze. And as I'd always been incapable of resisting him, in the end, with a sigh, I consented.

"Nothing. You'd better get some rest, you need it…"

Lenny stared at him persistently for several seconds and then slipped docilely under the covers. Soon weariness got the better of him. Hermin stayed where he was, contemplating the boy in his sleep.

11

SONG OF THE SPIRITS
OVER THE WATERS

For two days, Lenny's fever never left him. Despite being wrapped up in warm blankets and lying close to the blazing fire, he kept shivering. Periods of torpor alternated with moments of agitation, during which he was practically delirious, addressing Hermin in German and playing a piano made of air, as though interpreting music known to him alone. At times, his respiratory passages seemed obstructed and he was left gasping for breath; at other times, he would try to hum bits of melody in a broken voice, but those efforts would always end abruptly, and he'd lie there, looking undone, fists clenched against his chest, panting from pain.

The young composer didn't take his eyes off him. Hermin felt as powerless as he had in the past, but these present days were the worst he'd known in his life. Lenny's illness, the impossibility of taking any sort of action, their permanently cramped quarters—which compelled him to watch the young man's suffering uninterruptedly—oppressed Hermin to a nearly unbearable degree, and he was surprised to find that the similar ordeal ten years earlier had left him with what was almost a tender memory, a recollection of days that were precarious, sure, but filled with such intimacy, such trust, such *surrender* that he couldn't stop himself, whenever he called them to mind, from thinking about a lost Paradise.

Some days later, I ran into Iris at the Conservatory. We hadn't seen each other for a month. The boy's illness had required all my attention; my absence had doubtless surprised her. And so, when she approached me, the concern she felt was mingled with resentment.

To keep from going mad, and to occupy his days while remaining close to Lenny's side, he'd begun to compose again, with a sort of fever that seemed to emanate directly from the boy's body and to be communicated to him, to Hermin, by some spell—as if their vital substances had found themselves linked together, and the only way to keep the young man's alive were to transmute it into music. The *Homage to Schubert* was under way again; the work, which as recently as the previous day had seemed to be at a standstill, suddenly started growing as though of its own volition, and Hermin, panting, synchronized his breathing with Lenny's and wrote at full speed, which was barely fast enough for him to sketch out all the ideas that came to him, the intermingled themes, the haunting repetitions of Schubertian motifs. Perhaps the spur of pain and the sense that time was running out were the way by which he could find poor Franz's inspiration again and respond to him now, across the ages, to him who had turned out one masterpiece after another toward the end of his life: To compose with a sense of great urgency, was that not to follow a path traced by the very greatest? Hermin thought fleetingly about his brilliant older colleague Olivier Greif, whose premature death had occurred three years previously, and who in the final years of his existence had produced some of the musical masterworks of the twentieth century. But Hermin knew only too well that it wasn't his own death that he feared...

I gave her a summary of recent events. She made no comment. I thought about what Lenny had asked me to do, but I didn't know how to broach the subject. In the end, I opted for the most cowardly solution: I tried to work on her pity, betting that what she'd refuse to do for the boy she would do for me.

"*How are you going to justify your absences to the administration?*" *she asked opportunely.*

"*I don't know. In any case, I'm pretty sure I'm going to have to quit the Conservatory...*"

"*You can't be serious!*"

Nevertheless, little by little, Lenny's health improved, even though he still looked as exhausted as ever. His fever had gone down, and his condition was in no way comparable to what it had been during the days immediately following their mad night. And so Hermin could envision going back down to the Pommier Chenin, where they would at least be more comfortable, and where a physician, in the unlikely event that he could find one in this wilderness, might be induced to visit the patient. One morning, just as he was about to offer this suggestion, the young man anticipated him in a way Hermin couldn't have foreseen. His eyes stubbornly fixed on the portion of forest visible through the pavilion's window, Lenny suddenly declared, all in one breath, "I would like to go out. Walk…"

His features were drawn into a look of something like painful expectation, which had nothing to do with his illness. The yearning for snow lit up his eyes, and it seemed that his entire body aspired only to return to the landscape it had issued from—like a traveler painted by Friedrich and barbarously cut out of his canvas, trying in spite of everything to regain his rightful place in the scene.

"In that case, let's go back to the Pommier Chenin. The walk will get your circulation going—"

"I was thinking about a real walk."

Hermin, struck speechless, considered him for a while and then said, "Well, that's just not reasonable!"

The moment Hermin uttered those words, he realized how absurd they were. When had the boy ever worried about being *reasonable*? Ten years previously, the very word would make him jump; he'd rebel against his older friend's good sense and cling to his own resolutions all the more firmly. As far as that characteristic was concerned, Hermin had no doubt that Lenny remained unchanged...

"I do not care about that... Hermin, please..."

Now he was looking at his friend with pleading eyes, like an imploring child, and Hermin, as always, felt his resistance weakening in the face of that silent prayer.

"That *Wasserfall* you talked about, it is near here, yes?"

Hermin nodded, reluctantly—and then blurted out, "So you see yourself climbing rocks and sinking in snow up to your knees?"

His eyes hard with obstinacy, balking more childishly than a child at every common-sense argument, Lenny pretended not to have heard the objection. He was already on his feet and putting on his coat; his movements were unsteady, his steps uncertain, but the resolution that seemed to activate him was far superior to his body's weakness, and he was one of those persons who, once beset by thirst, cared for nothing else until that thirst was quenched. Hermin slowly erased one last measure, laid aside his pencil, and put away the score he was working on; then he followed the boy, who was opening the door of the pavilion.

I made her see the precariousness of my situation, my increasing difficulty in coping with my expenses, the burden of Lenny and his sick aunt. I was left with no choice, I had to work full-time.

"Maybe you could scare up a grant or something like that…"

"I've thought about it, but I don't meet the requirements!"

The winding path that led into the woods was just wide enough for the two of them to walk abreast. After some hesitation, Hermin gave Lenny his arm, and without a word the boy leaned against him.

For a long moment they remained silent, too absorbed in looking around them. Although Hermin knew the place by heart, he never tired of contemplating, from one winter to the next, the frosted undergrowth, the snow-covered woodpiles, the dark rocks. Above all else, he loved discovering, around one or another random bend in the path, frozen ponds that continued to reflect, imperfectly, the shabby barriers of wood or wire that bordered them, and he loved to approach such a pond and admire, captured in its ice, bubbles of air more sparkling than a set of diamonds. He felt that he was entering an enchanted country, and he cared little whether it was hostile or friendly, provided it let itself be discovered by the eyes of its visitor—for that was where it really was, he thought, the Schubertian *Aufenthalt** with its "rushing stream" and its "roaring forest," *"rauschender Strom, brausender Wald…"*

"I should never have come back," Lenny abruptly murmured.

---

* "Resting abode," "stopping place."

You could tell from his remote stare that what he'd just managed to declare was the result of a long thought process he'd been following parallel to their hike. Hermin suddenly felt cold inside his chest. "Maybe that's just because…you know, this place, the winter…I can see how all that might seem a little sinister…" he ventured, without any very clear idea of what he was saying. "Maybe things would have been different if I'd come to you, to see you in Paris…"

The boy smiled, in a way. "You would not have come to Paris. Not for me."

"How do you know?" the young composer replied, shrugging his shoulders.

But he knew his friend was right. He had never really tried to reconnect with the boy—contenting himself with waiting, forever and ever, for Fate to knock on his door. He would no doubt have waited in vain ten years longer…

"Hermin! You're ruining your studies and wasting your musical talent to help this…kid!"

"He's a great musician, it would be a crime to hinder his progress!"

"You're not Abbé Pierre! If he's really got a gift, there are other people who can help him!"

"But he doesn't want anybody's help but mine!"

The moment I uttered those words, I realized how completely absurd they were.

"And besides," Lenny went on, "this place here is very fine, that's not the problem... it could be in a Christmas story..."

He made a gesture to indicate their surroundings. The slopes were covered with an opalescent coat, and only here and there did patches of dark rock appear. A world in black and white—a pianist's Paradise.

"Imagine... we could have... gone hiking, and then talked, listened to music, together... We could have read scores, and practiced four-hands piano pieces, and played your compositions, *zusammen*,* and in the evening..."

He seemed to be lost in a waking dream. Perhaps he'd even forgotten that Hermin was at his side.

"'Between us two the winter cruel thus passed peacefully / Watching her fingers on the keyboard playing Schubert's *Trout*,'"† quoted the young composer, with a rather bitter smile on his lips.

Lenny nodded absently. The surrounding landscape surely had little to do with the ecstatic flame currently enlivening his eyes. Other images were offering themselves to him...

"Why are things not ever the way you want?" the boy whispered at last.

---

* "Together."

† Louis Aragon (from his poetry collection *Le Roman inachevé*, The Unfinished Romance).

At that moment, they came up against the trunk of a fallen tree, which barred their path. The tree was covered with snow and moss and, although lying on the ground, almost waist-high. It hadn't survived that last storm...

They consulted each other's eyes for a few instants, and the young composer was able to suppress, just in time, an "I told you so." To judge from Lenny's expression, he for his part had no intention of turning around and going back. As for going around the tree, it was out of the question. On the left, its branches were thoroughly fused with the tangled undergrowth, while one of the steepest slopes blocked their passage on the right. Hermin was the first to decide on climbing over the damp trunk. He stood tall and succeeded all at once in getting on top of the trunk, from which he overlooked the path and felt a forgotten joy, that of the child who climbs everywhere in order to feel as though he's dominating the world. It was as if the forest, recently but black and white, had suddenly adorned itself in other colors: the orange-tinted brown of the last leaves, the dark green of the moss, and even, in rare coruscations, the red pearls of holly. *Rise above*, he thought, with a hint of derision.

"*Listen, you can't possibly understand,*" *I said, dropping down a tone.*

"*Oh, yes, I can too understand! The truth is, this boy has gone to your head!*"

*"He hasn't gone to my head!" I replied, blushing hard.
"He needs me, that's all!"*

Then he remembered that Lenny was waiting for him to help him get over the obstacle. Hermin crouched down on the damp trunk, trying to keep his balance, which was rather a feat, and held out one hand to the boy so that he could pull himself up in his turn. At the cost of several efforts and one coughing fit, he succeeded. He sat on the trunk, heedless of the snow and the damp, and swung his legs a little in the empty air.

"In fact, I think I knew," he said after an instant, resuming the conversation as if nothing had interrupted them.

"Knew what?"

"That this is not a Christmas story. Too beautiful…"

"Then why come back?" Hermin said, deciding to jump down from the trunk.

The question had burst out before he could stop it, and he inwardly cursed himself. And yet…to deny that this very question had been obsessing him for weeks would have been to demonstrate colossal bad faith—or unparalleled blindness.

Lenny, still sitting on the tree, bent his head down toward Hermin. He gazed at him for a few seconds, and Hermin thought he was going to have to hear, once again, a reply along the lines of "Are you really asking that question?" or some similar evasion. But against all expectation, the boy in his turn let himself slip off the tree to the ground and began to hum, almost inaudibly, a catchy little melody, while never taking his attentive eyes off his friend. For an instant, Hermin thought he was going mad, but then he recognized the tune in question.

"That's 'Illusion,' right? *'Täuschung'*?"

Lenny nodded and murmured the words:

Ach, wer wie ich so elend ist
Gibt gern sich hin der bunten List,
Die hinter Eis und Nacht und Graus
Ihm weist ein helles, warmes Haus,
Und eine liebe Seele drin—
Nur Täuschung ist für mich Gewinn!*

That was German Hermin could understand, because he'd worked on the lied for an examination in his singing class, years before—and the text made his heart ache. The lines echoed so perfectly Schubert's own words, which Hermin had discovered by chance:

Imagine a man...whose brightest hopes have turned to naught, to whom the joys of love and friendship offer nothing but torment...

---

* "Ah, who so wretched is as I / Falls gladly for the cheerful lie / That says, past ice and night and dread / A bright house waits, a cozy bed, / And a beloved soul therein— / Only illusion lets me win!"

"Lenny…"

Hermin fell silent. What to say, in any case? He was sick at heart, he too, from watching his friend go about his own destruction, gnawed at by obscure torments, just as he suffered to hear his incessant coughing. In the one case as in the other, Hermin felt terribly helpless. Lenny was one of those who engaged in hand-to-hand combat with their demons— all alone.

The time had come for me to go for broke: "But you, you've got a grant…If you were willing to help us…I'd pay you back as soon as I could…"

She stared at me, unable to believe her ears. "My darling Hermin," she said sarcastically, "if I have a scholarship, it's because I need one! Contrary to what your pal may think, the parental manna doesn't fall on me!"

They resumed walking in silence. They still had to cross a little footbridge that spanned a mountain torrent. The water, which Hermin knew as crystalline in springtime, was carrying along such a quantity of mud that its current color was chestnut brown—although dotted with white foam.

"The Rhine must have been like this when Schumann threw himself into it," said Lenny, leaning over the guardrail.

"A little wider, surely," Hermin joked, even though the remark made him shiver—neither Hermin himself nor anyone else but Lenny would have come up with such an analogy.

They continued on their way to the waterfall. This was certainly the most delicate stage of their hike. In order to follow the torrent flowing through the little valley, they had to negotiate some steep slopes, passing from rock to rock, taking care not to slip on the damp, glistening surfaces, and clinging to tree branches when the incline became too abrupt. Of course, there was no very great danger, and a child could have accomplished the exploit, but Lenny was starting to tire, even though he didn't say a word about it, and Hermin couldn't help being worried by this. How were they going to be able to get back to the Pommier Chenin when the time came?

"Iris…if you really think it would be a waste for me to drop out…"

I hated myself for what I was doing, but the young woman wasn't fooled. She said, "Hermin, if I was sure it would help you, I'd agree! But I know very well what's going to happen… You're going to keep on sacrificing yourself, and Lenny will be the one who goes to the Conservatory!"

They advanced cautiously. Hermin went first, carefully seeking the safest places to step on and then helping Lenny to follow him. Lenny clung to his friend's arm with all his meager strength and walked precisely in Hermin's footsteps, as if doing so would guarantee the safety of his progress. At no time did he ask if they would get there soon—his pride would have suffered too much. They could hear, more and more clearly, the roar of the water, which no doubt sufficed to give the boy enough courage to proceed. Finally, after having passed over some rocks like monsters asleep for so long that moss had covered them completely, they arrived within sight of the cascade.

The deluge of water came tumbling down in front of them, spattering the rock where they were standing as foam spatters the prow of a ship. Although the waterfall was of no great height, it had the force of a mighty stream—all the more so since the recent storm had no doubt swollen the few tributaries that fed the torrent—and was in any case imposing enough to take the breath away from anyone who contemplated it from its midpoint. And the two hikers did in fact find the spectacle breathtaking. Instinctively, they drew closer to each other and stared without speaking at that emanation of the *Sturm und Drang*, that *Wasserfall*, more Romantic than Rimbaudian, in which they both seemed to recognize an echo of Schubert's *Song of the Spirits over the Waters*:

The pure stream
Leaps from the high,
Steep rock face...
Should cliffs protrude,
Deflecting its fall,
Then angrily foaming
It pours down by steps
Into the abyss...

They gradually passed from wonder to fascination. An inspiring wind seized them and carried them off to other worlds. All language was abolished, ceding its place to raw emotion, to that unthinking, unfettered *presence*, and it seemed to them that they themselves were dissolved in the waterfall, that they too became the torrential water, the rapids, the spray bounding off the rocks. The *Wasserfall* married them.

She came closer to me and fixed her eyes on mine. "Listen to what I'm telling you, Hermin," she said, separately enunciating each word. "This snot-nosed brat is going to ruin your life, and when you finally realize that, it will be too late!"

How long they stayed there, deafened by the roaring water, Hermin couldn't have said. Pressed against each other, they seemed to be feeling, after so many days, the same emotion at the same time—and that thought took their breath away as surely as the cascade did. The young composer felt Lenny's head resting on his shoulder, the younger man's soft breath against his cheek. A knot formed in Hermin's throat, and he began to think that if the two of them had really dissolved in the cascade, as he'd imagined a moment before, then they would have formed a single "spirit over the waters."

He felt Lenny collapse against him all of a sudden—he turned around—the spell was broken.

"The Malgoutte..." the boy murmured, his strength gone. "I am glad I saw it."

"This was crazy," said Hermin, his tone no longer reproachful.

With those words, she turned on her heel and left me standing there. I didn't move for a long time, staring at the door she'd come out of. We would never see each other again.

He crouched down beside the boy. Whatever awkwardness, whatever resentment he might have felt over the course of the past several weeks had disappeared, as though washed away by the cascade and its cleansing surge. All that remained was affection, like what he used to feel for him in former days, and the distress of seeing him in such a state.

"No worry, it will be all right," Lenny breathed. "I am just tired…"

Hermin nodded, unable to speak. Then, delicately, he passed one arm under the boy's shoulder and helped him get to his feet.

"Do you think you can walk now?"

After a pause, his friend nodded. They set out on the way back to the Pommier Chenin, while the shadows lengthened and the landscape took on a reddish hue.

12

"THERE WAS A KING
OF THULE ..."

Night was falling when they reached the Pommier Chenin. Hermin quickly set a log afire in the hearth, located some blankets, and dried off Lenny's hair, which was still dripping with melted snow. They huddled together in front of the fireplace. Then the young composer offered to prepare some mulled wine. While Hermin went about this task, Lenny stayed where he was, unmoving, staring at nothing. Perhaps he was contemplating, through the window in the Great Room, the last lights of the day—the *Abendrot*, literally the "evening red," the scarlet sunset glow   seconded by the flickering flames, which an interior music, by Schubert or Richard Strauss, seemed to enhance with a thousand bursts of light. There are some people—these two were among them—for whom the world is the reflection of art.

Naturally, I had to apologize to my professors for my absence. I decided to start with Monsieur Guillemin, who taught harmony.

When Hermin, carrying two metal cups, went back to his friend, he couldn't help being struck by the spectacle of the light playing on his face. Instead of coloring the pallor of his features, the tawny flashes seemed to be superimposed on them, as a mask is superimposed on the face of the person wearing it, and Lenny's ashen complexion only stood out all the more sharply, like the wax of a burning candle.

Without a word, Hermin poured out the mulled wine. The boy moved a little, as though hauled out of his torpor. Examining the metal goblet in his hand, he half sang, half murmured, with a sort of distant smile,

"...*Dem sterbend seine Buhle*
Einen goldnen Becher gab..."*

It seemed to Hermin he was shivering a little.

Monsieur Guillemin was the nicest professor on the Conservatory faculty. Of course, had it not been for his prodigious knowledge, the institution would no doubt have tried to oust him from his job, for he failed to conform, strictly speaking, to the "house style." He was so constantly distracted that you

---

* "...To whom his dying lady / A golden goblet gave..."

might have said he'd come from another planet. As he never refused to admit anyone into his classes, they were always filled with a joyous crowd of students who had no business there; one day some joker had even hung a sign on the door of the classroom: "Open to all, space permitting."

Lenny began once again to hum the melody of the "King of Thule," now gazing fixedly at the tin goblet, now distracted by a branch beating against the darkened window. As for Hermin, the mighty roar of the waterfall was still resounding in his ears, and he tried to recapture the sudden feeling of communion, so fleeting, that had seized him that afternoon and had, for a brief moment, reunited them.

> *"…Die Augen gingen ihm über,*
> *So oft er trank daraus…"**

By what miracle, by what obscure wonder, had he been able to feel again, so suddenly, and with the weight of evidence, that all the barriers between them had been destroyed? And why couldn't he bring that feeling to life again now?

His musical tastes were likewise, for a Conservatory professor, most unusual. Everyone knew the high value he placed on the work of Francis Poulenc and Erik Satie—he had some

---

* "…The tears welled up in his eyes / Whenever he drank from it…"

serious temperamental affinities with the latter—and in the
disputes that agitated the small world of contemporary music
and musicians, he resolutely supported those who were called
the "neotonals" (or, more spitefully, the "tonalitarians"). He
loved to ask us, "So, my children, this cadence: mānor or
mījor?"

As Lenny was again refilling his goblet with mulled
wine, the pot nearly slipped from his hand, and several drops
spattered the hearth tiles. A moment later, he stretched out
his arm to put his empty goblet back on the edge of the
fireplace—but didn't complete the movement. Hermin
rushed to him while the goblet was still rolling around on
the floor. He heard himself saying some incoherent words
to which the young man made no reply; he was fighting for
air. Hermin led him to an armchair. He leaned on its back
for an instant, trying to recover his breath. When he raised
his head, a thin trickle of blood was running down his chin.

Hermin shuddered. Once again, he considered his
friend's exhausted features, his grayish lips, his almost violet pupils, and he couldn't help recalling that other distraught
face, the one he had never stopped thinking about. Now Constance struck him as the fateful "double," the doppelgänger
who takes possession of bodies and drains them of their
substance...He rejected that vision: how many times had
he caught her, toward the end, spitting clotted blood into her
handkerchief while doing her utmost to put up a brave front...

All that notwithstanding, no one should believe that his course was easy, or his teaching lax. Beyond the shadow of a doubt, it was in his class that we learned the most, provided that we attentively followed every single thing he said, including the smallest digressions. He applied the same care to correcting a routine exercise as to critiquing a string quartet composed in Debussy's style. So I'd missed the experience of attending his classes, and I looked forward with pleasure to seeing him again. In general, Guillemin didn't remember his students' faces, but since he found me reasonably talented and I'd been taking his courses for two years, he had eventually noticed me.

"Well, it's young Pareyre!" he said when he saw me. "You haven't picked up your last exercise, I believe…"

"Peyre, Monsieur. No," I muttered, without pointing out that I'd also failed to turn in the following exercise.

He received my apologies and explanations benevolently but seemed to retain only one element of my little speech: "The friend you've been taking care of—you say he's a pianist?"

I replied in the affirmative but revealed that he wasn't a Conservatory student.

"Was he the one you played those Beethoven sonatas with last Dooombor?"

Evidently, he remembered our performance at a sort of "Schubertiade" given by students—not even a real concert— to which he'd been invited. When my reply was again positive, his face lit up.

"I looked for him among the students…That boy was tremendously talented…I would have liked to hear what he could do solo…"

"As soon as he's fully recovered, he'd be delighted to play for you," I assured the professor, hardly able to believe my ears.

Lenny wiped the blood from his chin with the back of his hand and then returned to his armchair.

"You are thinking about Constance," he murmured. "I was wondering when you would understand."

Constance was a consumptive, and he himself…

"So when you got here…" said Hermin, unable to go on.

"I was already sick," the boy said with a sad smile, finishing his sentence for him.

I already knew that once Guillemin had singled out a musician, he would do everything in his power to promote his cause. His acquaintance included a number of influential people, and he wouldn't hesitate to make introductions or provide concert opportunities. A friend of mine named Natcha had profited from his generosity, and her career had progressed very quickly. I was dazzled by such prospects.

He started coughing again. While his chest rose and fell spasmodically, he added: "Forgive me…for hiding this from you. I did not dare…I was afraid of how you would react…"

Hermin put a hand on his shoulder. His shaking subsided a little. Hermin asked, "But why didn't you get medical help?"

Lenny silently stared at him for a moment. Now his eyes seemed empty. "That is my business," he said.

As was his habit, Hermin found no other recourse than to lose his temper: "That's so irresponsible!"

"Maybe."

Hermin made no reply. He felt himself plunging into genuine despair. His eyes fell on the Zimmermann, the silent witness to the whole scene.

In fact, several days later, I received an offer from a certain M. Devère, who gave promising young artists the opportunity to perform in public. When I showed Lenny the letter, he was as stunned as I was, and in spite of his still-obvious weakness, I couldn't dissuade him from immediately sitting down at the piano again.

"Lenny...is that why you gave up the piano?"

The boy nodded and drew the famous *Diapason* article from his pocket. "If you are interested, there is this..."

Hermin snatched the page but wasn't able to read it. The lines danced before his eyes, intermingling like boughs. All he could gather was that the article's subject was a recital whose first half had featured Chopin's "Funeral March" sonata, and whose second half had been canceled.

"I...I almost fainted, there onstage, while I was playing...It was the first time...In the intermission, the impresario saw how I could not stand up..." Lenny explained in a faltering voice. "I had no choice than to stop..."

Our situation, which until then I had considered almost desperate, was on the verge of changing radically.

The candle in one of the fluted candlesticks that Hermin had left in place since the boy's return finished burning itself out. Mechanically, Hermin scratched with a fingernail at the wax that had collected and hardened in the grooves. "I'll take you to the hospital tomorrow," he said.

Lenny clenched a fist on the armrest of his chair. "Never."

"You think I'm giving you a choice?"

"We will have an accident."

Spoken by anybody else, that sentence would have constituted a simple warning related to the snowdrifts, the icy roads, the possibility of more bad weather to come; in that boy's mouth, the words sounded like a threat. Hermin thought he was capable of sending them into a ditch...

"You're out of your mind, Lenny. From now on, *I'll* be the one who makes the decisions."

And, paying no attention to his friend's protests, Hermin grabbed him under one arm and dragged him to his bedroom upstairs. Too weak to struggle, Lenny was compelled to obey. Climbing the stairs was a fresh ordeal. The boy was again racked with coughing and could barely stand. They were obliged to stop on the landing, for without his friend's support, Lenny would have given up before the end. Hermin had plenty of time to curse himself, furious at his own failure to act sooner, at his having allowed, whether irresponsibly or blindly, the state of Lenny's health to deteriorate to this point.

But while he was tucking Lenny in like a child, the memory of the long nights he'd spent watching over the boy ten years before came back to him in a flood, and he was overcome by a violent feeling of affection, the same as what he'd felt when he faced the waterfall.

"Lenny…" he whispered. "I promise everything's going to be all right, I promise…"

The young man looked at him with feverish eyes and, not without some difficulty, smiled. Although Lenny was already half-asleep, Hermin thought he could still hear him murmuring "…*Trank letzte Lebensglut*…"* before he sank into complete unconsciousness.

---

* "…Drank up his life's last glow…"

13

GUTE NACHT

The following day, Hermin went into action at dawn, determined to drive his friend to Renaison, where he could be properly taken care of. Planning to stay in a hotel as long as might be necessary, Hermin packed a bag, closed all the Pommier Chenin's shutters, and turned off the water. Then he went upstairs to awaken Lenny.

His room was empty.

Hermin stood still for a few seconds, dumbfounded. The bed was made, and the boy's meager baggage lay in a corner under the portrait of Schubert. Hermin ran down the stairs.

The Great Room was, naturally, empty too; Hermin had passed through it a few minutes earlier...Alarmed by a fearful suspicion, he opened the front door. In the courtyard, he could clearly distinguish footprints leading away from the house and not yet effaced by the morning snow.

Lenny wanted to announce the good news to his aunt without delay and even to ask if she thought it would be possible for her to attend the concert. Of course, Constance didn't know that the boy had been sick—we hadn't seen her for a month—but now his recovery was so far advanced that she wouldn't suspect anything if we went and paid her a visit.

Hermin went back upstairs to the boy's room. Had he taken any of his things with him? No, everything seemed to be in its place—including the musical scores purloined ten years previously and now lying in plain sight on the night table. On the top of the pile, as if by chance, the score of *Winterreise*, and slipped inside it but still sticking out far enough to be seen, a sheet of paper covered with shaky handwriting. Holding his breath, Hermin pulled out the page and began to read.

Hermin,

    This letter, I have wanted to write it for a long time, and I should have it written long ago. I should have it written ten years ago, in fact, but I did not dare. I dare now because I have nothing to lose. My only hope is that you will not hate me too much, afterward, or in any case not more than at this moment. You promised.

    So, I am leaving, and this time you will not see me again. Gute Nacht: "Fremd bin ich eingezogen,

fremd zieh' ich wieder aus."* *In fact, I am begging
you: do not look for me. You know, I was all the
same happy to spend these last days here. I have
always dreamed about it, this snow, and these
paths:* "Nun ist die Welt so trübe, der Weg gehüllt
in Schnee..."†

*(Just think, it was you who introduced me to
that!)*

*So, I have no desire to finish in a hospital.
I prefer to walk to the end, to see the mountain
streams, and the dark, dark forests, the houses
almost ruined with just a little smoke above the
roof—maybe, if I reach the mountaintop, I will
be able to see the chimney of the Pommier Chenin?
Yesterday, at the waterfall—I would really liked for
this to finish like that. But all the same, before, you
must to have known.*

"Wenn ich dich lieb habe, was geht's dich an?"
(Goethe)

*"If I love you, is that any of your business?"—
there, that is what I thought!*

Hermin, you were mein Bruder, mein Vater—*I
would liked for you to be* meine Liebe,‡ *but no. It*

---

* "Good Night: 'A stranger came I hither, / A stranger go I hence.'"

† "Now is the world so gloomy, / The way entombed in snow."

‡ "My brother," "my father"—"my love."

is why I came back. Before, I thought to be a child
for you, it was normal that nothing happens. Now,
I am twenty-seven, and so I thought this time will
be different, maybe you have understood while I
am absent, or maybe I will can talk to you...I told
myself if you love me, I go to a doctor—but if not,
it is useless. Too bad. Do not blame yourself, it is
not your fault. It is my choice. And then there is my
cowardness: maybe if I had spoken before...

All the same, how did you do to not see? Or
then you knew but you said nothing? I often asked
myself the question. What a pity, I will not ever
know. Meine letzte Hoffnung, my last hope: that
you are like me and you do not dare either.

I cannot even remember anymore since when I
love you. So, no fond memories or discussions about
that. In any case, "it is my business," not true?

And thanks all the same, for everything. My
best moments, they were with you, in the garret
when we played piano for four hands or when you
showed me how to make trills, and then obviously
Schubert   you know Leopold Kupelwieser's drawing when Schubert is young? I carried it around
for years, I think he looks like you. Or maybe I am
dreaming. Anyway, it was better to play for you
alone than the Salle Pleyel. It is for you, just for

you, that I became pianist (you have never looked at the Widmungen* on my discs?).

At last. Now you know, nothing else to add. No more words, no more music. But yes, all the same— finish the Homage to Schubert for me. That is all.

I love you.

Lenny

P.S. Here are your scores. I held them because your writing was on them.

Hermin put down the letter and felt tears spring up in his eyes.

He had willfully deluded himself for well over a decade; he'd baptized their relationship with a name that didn't suit it; he'd persisted in that lie for months, for years. And now, he wasn't sure of anything—or rather...

And so one morning, we set out for the sanatorium in my dented old car. Lenny was very impatient, and also very worried: he was naturally wondering about the state of his aunt's health. Would it be improved by his new standard of living? Personally, I doubted it, but of course I hid my skepticism from the boy.

...He knew that he'd loved Lenny more than anything or anyone, but he'd thought he loved him like a friend, like

---

* "Dedications."

a brother, like a father sometimes—not like a lover. Except, perhaps... The evening of the snowstorm, what had he felt as he struggled to save the boy? Desire, no doubt, a passion both sudden and violent that he had very quickly done his best to forget... And then yesterday, at the waterfall, the boundless affection that had surged up in him while he held the boy close... What a fool, ah, what a fool! Furtively, he thought about a novella by Stefan Zweig whose title, for reasons he wasn't clear about, had always fascinated him: *Confusion of Feelings*. There was also a sentence in Roger Peyrefitte's novel *Special Friendships*, the book of his teen-age years, whose words had printed themselves indelibly on his brain, forming the storyline of a prophecy he hadn't been able to interpret: "Know this, if you still wanted to deny it: the name of our friendship is love."

We found the old lady in a white-walled room, irreproach-ably clean but absolutely empty, without any sort of decora-tion. One way or another, you could tell that the people who sojourned in that room weren't destined to remain there long. My heart ached at the sight of Constance, lost in the middle of a bed too large for her, staring into the void. One could well won-der what she did with her days, she who spoke practically no French and had no access to German books. There was nothing and no one to distract her from her painful memories...

He made up his mind at once. Introspection, remorse, "personal pathos"—that could all come later. He thrust the letter into his pocket and leapt down the stairs, four at a time. Somewhere in the mountains, Lenny was walking, coughing, and despite what he may have said, cursing him, Hermin, for having caused his ruin. But maybe he shouldn't be thinking such thoughts. The important thing was to find Lenny as quickly as possible and take him to Renaison. Repentance could be postponed...

She welcomed us so gratefully it broke my heart. Of course, we were the first visitors able to distract her...Lenny hugged her cautiously: she seemed so frail, so pale, that one false move could have broken her. I could see the blue veins in her wrist showing through the diaphanous skin. She was even thinner than before.

The car bumped along the rough road that led away from the house. For a moment, Hermin feared he'd get bogged down in the mud, and he could feel his heart beating faster. Then he reached the main highway and could breathe a little. But which way to go? He was on the border between two departments, Loire and Allier, and he knew that the roads in Loire were generally better cleared than those in Allier. However, wasn't it more probable that the boy would have chosen to go to the station in Les Hormières, in spite of the glare ice and the snowdrifts? A curious sensation of déjà vu seized the young composer as he turned onto the highway. But this time, he knew Lenny wouldn't have sought refuge in the pavilion. All Hermin could do was to crisscross the countryside again. Conditions were more favorable than they'd been the previous week, and he was sure that Lenny, now even weaker, couldn't have gotten very far—which was hardly a reassuring thought.

They started speaking to each other in German. Of course, I couldn't understand what they were saying, but I had no difficulty discerning Lenny's anxiety. Constance replied in one breath, her voice cracking. The decline in her health was all too apparent.

It suddenly occurred to Hermin to consider the clues contained in Lenny's letter. He talked about reaching the mountaintop and looking down on the Pommier Chenin in the valley below...But would he have had the strength to climb up the slope when it would have been so much easier to descend toward Arfeuilles?

Thus Hermin began a desperate quest through the countryside. The sky was completely overcast and milky white, and the fog, which seemed like a halo rising up from lands gripped by the cold, shrouded the hills, erased their contours, clasped them in a vaporous embrace. There were no hikers to be seen on the gravel roads or the iced-over paths. The silent, solitary countryside was holding its breath at the approach of the bitterest cold. As for Hermin, he kept driving along, gnawed at by the dread of arriving too late, of not finding the boy, or...He tried to silence the voices echoing in his head:

"It is why I came back…"

"I told myself if you love me, I go to a doctor—but if not, it is useless…"

"All the same, how did you do to not see?"

Yes, what had he done so as not to see, so as not to want to see?

She was seized by a sudden coughing fit more violent than anything we'd heard until then. Bent in half on her bed, she looked as though something inside her were tearing her to pieces. Lenny stood up in panic, blurted out a few words, and hurried from the room in search of a nurse.

While he was passing near a muddy path that disappeared into a forest, the sound of voices revealed that he wasn't alone. He stopped, got out, and ran to a clearing that two woodcutters were making. When he asked them if they had perhaps seen a young man passing through, they shook their heads. Hermin went back to the car and continued on his way.

He obtained the same result some distance away, from an old woman who was feeding her chickens. For a moment, he thought that Lenny might have sought refuge at some farm, but then he rejected that idea. Anybody with good sense would have immediately taken him to a hospital—which was precisely what the boy wanted to avoid…

Hermin arrived at the hamlet known as Les Biefs. There, behind the former public school, a path led through the woods and then ended on a deforested slope, from which one could view the whole valley, all the way to Arfeuilles. Had the boy really wanted to see the Pommier Chenin's chimney, he might have taken that path…But was he at all familiar with the vantage point it offered? Sure, for several weeks he'd hiked the Bourbonnais Mountains—which didn't necessarily mean he'd discovered everything…

Just to be sure, Hermin parked his car and plunged into the woods, rapidly reaching the summit of the hill, from where he could overlook the valley. The view was truly like a Bruegel painting, with little roads winding among snow-covered plots of land, thin groves of bare-branched trees, a few frozen ponds, and some farmhouses huddled together, as though for warmth, around a bell tower. Patches of mist mingled with the plumes of smoke rising from the hamlets.

No trace of Lenny.

I took Lenny's place at her side, as helpless as he. I grasped her hand, which was so pale that it seemed transparent. "Everything's going to be all right…Don't worry…It'll be all right…" I stammered, overcome

After a few moments, her coughing calmed down a little. She tried to sit up, her back against her pillows, and taking advantage of our brief time alone, she whispered a few words that I had trouble understanding, so weak was her voice: "Thank you. For…what you do for him…"

He was about to turn around and go back when he noticed a thin ribbon of silver, snaking along the opposite side of the valley.

"Yesterday, at the waterfall—I would really liked for this to finish like that..."

It was his only other clue. Hermin had discounted it because he thought it highly improbable that the boy would have had the strength to try a second assault on the Malgoutte. Now he wasn't so sure.

He retraced his steps down the path, reached his car, and got back on the road.

Then she added: "After I die...do not stop helping him... please..."

There we were. My heart sank painfully. "You're not going to die, Constance, you..."

I broke off. Lenny was coming back, preceded by a nurse.

Now that he'd given himself a destination, Hermin drove faster. A sort of melody repeated itself obsessively in his mind, spurring him on—one of Schubert's *Moments musicaux*, perhaps No. 4 in C-sharp minor, with its perpetual-motion opening section, but he couldn't have sworn to it. The important thing was that this music was accompanying his quest, supporting him, and above all preventing him from thinking about anything except the ribbon of highway rolling out before him; Lenny had played the piece, as Hermin remembered, after several months of piano lessons, and he'd played it perfectly, despite his tendency to accelerate, a habit it had cost him some difficulty to break, and...No, he shouldn't think about that...

The latter examined Constance and then decided to take me aside, under the pretext of leaving aunt and nephew alone. He told me nothing I hadn't already guessed: the old woman's life was nearing its end; she could die from one moment to the next. He promised to notify me.

There was an inn near the Malgoutte where woodcutters between two clearing jobs would come to eat *pâté de pommes de terre* (potato pie). Hermin went inside and asked if anyone had seen the boy. For the first time, the answers were affirmative: yes, he'd even stopped there, looking exhausted, he'd drunk a glass of wine before continuing on his way...No, no one had tried to stop him, why would anybody do that? An old man added that he'd seen the boy start up the path to the waterfall. Hermin's heart began to beat harder. His intuition had been correct.

He ran out of the inn and got on the path, calling out to Lenny. A light wind was moaning in the trees, exhaling a cry like a child's, sickly and almost sorrowful. Hermin couldn't help thinking about the falsely reassuring words of Goethe's poem "Erlkönig," about the forest goblin called "Erl-king," "King of the Alders"—

Be calm, stay quiet, my child so dear,
Wind rustling dead leaves, that's what you hear...

—words with which the father, to whom the Erl-king's charms
remain indiscernible, tries to soothe his frightened child...

As he'd done the previous day, Hermin crossed the
footbridge over the torrent, climbed up the slope, clambered
over the trunk of the fallen tree. With every step, it seemed
to him more and more impossible that Lenny had succeeded
in reaching the cascade.

*When we returned to the room, Lenny and his aunt were
deep in a quite animated discussion. I was astonished to see
that Constance's eyes looked brighter, and that she seemed
suddenly more alert. Without a doubt, the boy had just told
her the good news. Her reaction was surprising. She appeared
torn between a feeling of legitimate pride and a sorrow that
showed through the depths of her dark irises—regret at not
being able to attend the concert, or something more secret?*

And then he spotted him, lying on the ground a few
paces from a frozen pond, his head resting on melted snow.
Hermin ran to his side.

"Lenny," he murmured in a strangled voice.

The boy moved a little. A puddle of crystalline water
had soaked his shirt, which bore traces of faded bloodstains.

*Our good-byes were distressing. She was surely aware
that she was seeing us for the last time. I don't know whether*

*Lenny sensed that as clearly as I did, but abandoning her in
such a place was in any case a torment for him.*

"Viel Glück," *she murmured as we were leaving.*

That "good luck" wish was her last farewell.

Lenny opened his feverish eyes and recognized the person who had just knelt beside him. "*Du bist wiedergekommen...*"* he said in a breath.

"*Ja,*" Hermin replied, smiling weakly.

The he slipped an arm under the boy's shoulders, lifted him off the ground, and carried him, as well as he could, back to the car. Lenny, half-conscious, put up no resistance. When the young composer pulled onto the road, the boy murmured something that sounded like "*Danke.*"

---

* "You came back..."

14

PIANO SONATA, D. 959: ANDANTINO

They were looking at each other.

Hermin had assisted the young man out of the vehicle, helped him walk to the Great Room, and seated him on the sofa. Now they faced each other, holding their breath.

"Well?" Lenny finally said. "You found the letter?"

His voice was weak, its timbre almost broken, but the young composer had no trouble understanding him. He nodded.

"I'm so sorry," he added in one breath, not knowing whether those simple words were adequate to express everything he was feeling, but unable to come up with others.

Lenny nodded in his turn, as if to show that he understood. Then he said, "Just tell me...After all this time...Did you know, or not?"

"I think I avoided seeing."

"All right."

A period of silence followed. With a lump in his throat, Hermin cast his eyes down: the sight of the boy—his pallor, his hollow cheeks—was too painful for him.

"So you do not love me?" asked Lenny, speaking with effort.

Hermin raised his head. With this question, which could elicit but one response, the young man seemed to be calling for the final blow, as though compelled by the doleful desire to *lay bare*, once and for all, his life's devastation, to take its entire measure, with a sort of tragic joy—the elation of the man who admires, glinting in the light, the broadsword he's about to turn on himself.

The day of the concert finally arrived. I think I can say without being too mistaken that I was much more anxious than Lenny, and that the prospect of seeing him go out onto the stage terrified me. Of course, I knew his program was thoroughly prepared and his technique impeccable, but... suppose I was wrong? And what if the audience wasn't seduced, as I had been from the start, by the boy's gifts, by his luminous, fiery playing, by his excellence? To be sure, Lenny had already performed in a few concerts, but before ordinary, undemanding audiences. This time the stakes were higher, and I couldn't help thinking that Lenny's future career would partly depend on tonight's performance.

Hermin swallowed hard. What to say? He himself no longer knew exactly where he stood. In one sense, he had never loved anyone more than he loved the boy; but what kind of love was in question here? Oh, what wouldn't he have given, at that moment, to love Lenny as Lenny did him, to requite the feelings Lenny felt! To be able at last to reach accord, in the musical sense of the term, after so many years spent playing side by side, trying to mingle their respective songs without ever achieving real success, as if their souls had been the strings of two instruments, vibrating together, certainly, but in different keys... Ten years before, at the Conservatory, Hermin had studied polytonality with a certain jubilation. Now he aspired to nothing other than to rediscover the fullness of classical harmony and the *accord parfait*, the "perfect chord."

My fears mounted when he stepped onto the stage. I stood in the wings, gazing at his puny silhouette. The suit he had on was a bit too big for him—and with good reason, as he'd borrowed it from me—and I wondered how the devil a boy so frail could win over an audience. He barely greeted them, no doubt deeming such simpering a waste of time, and without bothering to take a deep breath, he flung himself headlong at the keyboard.

"Well?" said the boy when Hermin's silence dragged on.

A kind of trembling ran through his voice, as if the fact of not having received an immediate response to his question had engendered in him some new form of hope, against which he was now struggling with all his might.

For a few seconds, the young composer continued to hesitate, not knowing what to say or do, almost as lost as the person facing him. Then, practically in spite of himself, he elected to murmur, "I...I'd love to love you."

That evening, he was scheduled to play—how could I forget?—Schubert's Wanderer Fantasy, *followed by both of Brahms's piano* Rhapsodies *and a few of his* Intermezzi. *If I had entertained a fearful notion that Lenny would be paralyzed by stage fright and that those technically difficult pieces would suffer as a result, I was quickly disabused. He was one of those performers for whom the presence of an audience seemed instead to act as a stimulant, and he played his program with an energy, a verve I'd seldom seen him display before.*

"I see," said Lenny with a defeated smile.

Then he dropped back onto the sofa, as though drained of strength. Hermin resisted the urge to hide his face. A magic lantern seemed to be projecting before his eyes images that superimposed themselves on his perception of the supine boy, or rather, blurred his features and made them look younger, while the echoes of lost time resounded in Hermin's ears...

What to say, except that he worked wonders? By the apparent casualness of his playing, by his ability, while playing, to enter the music totally, oblivious of what surrounded him, he conquered the auditorium. Furthermore, my worries about his appearance on the stage had certainly been misguided: the angelic purity of his features supplanted his scrawny build in the audience's image of him and must have even, right from the start, gained the favor of a certain number. "The privileges of beauty are immense," said Cocteau. "It acts even on those who don't notice it."

He saw again, as in a kaleidoscope, the fifteen-year-old Lenny, who had entered the piano store for the first time, whom he'd surprised in the practice room at the Conservatory, who had waited for him in the rain, who had given his first recital while Constance lay dying...who had come, many years later, through the door of the Pommier Chenin...Lenny, his drawn features, his eyes, where a despair that Hermin hadn't wished to see showed through, his body, which was slowly being eaten away, offered up, so to speak, to his disease, as though sacrificed...

Guillemin and Devère had joined me in the wings. While Lenny was attacking the Fantasy's *third movement, my professor whispered to me, in a voice full of approbation, "Your instincts were decidedly correct. This young man will go far, I have no doubt."*

"He's got extraordinary potential, that's obvious from his sound," Devère said approvingly. He was evidently quite pleased with himself.

As well he should have been; the recital already seemed like a real success.

Suddenly, though not without difficulty, the young man sat up. His eyes locked on to Hermin's.

He stood up, leaned on the arm the young composer offered him, and with tottering steps undertook to traverse the few meters that separated the sofa from the piano. Understanding his intention, Hermin felt a blast of wind blow through him, a gust of mingled desire and anguish.

"Lenny, you can hardly stand up..."

"Oh, stop it... You have waited two months for this."

He sat at the piano, spent a few moments in silence, as though gathering his strength, and started to play.

The other two went back to their seats in the auditorium, and I was left alone in the wings, listening to Lenny. He was definitely outdoing himself. Back then, he already had at his command a palette of exceptional nuances—the fact of having been able to train on all the pianos in the store had perhaps contributed to that—and with the help of the acoustics in the hall, he managed to elicit from the big Steinway some sounds that were his alone.

Hermin's heart leapt when he heard the first thin, fragile notes of the melody reverberate in the darkness of the Great Room. Schubert. The Andantino movement of his second-to-last piano sonata. A piece that, more than any other, had decided his vocation. A piece that Lenny had discovered with him, and which he'd included on his first recording in memory of their "years of apprenticeship."

Once again, it seemed to Hermin that a phantom silhouette had come from the past, from the beginning, and taken the player's place, adopting his posture and his gestures. Lenny was still fifteen, he was sight-reading the score in the calm of the garret room, illuminated by an oblique light that threw his youthfully exultant features into relief, and Hermin was listening to him, unspeaking, perhaps with a premonition of what was to happen twelve years later, the clear jet gushing from a spring that had run dry, the resurrection of a song that had fallen silent...

Fragments of some sentences came back to him, sentences that he'd read several years before and that had etched themselves indelibly in his memory, like an obscure prophecy of the music that would be played, first behind the closed door of the garret room, and then in the heart of the numb and frozen countryside:

> We whom life frightens, whom the wind blows
> about at whim... we who waste ourselves in
> vain regrets, who postpone until later what was
> already impossible yesterday... we, the tender and
> childlike, we with vagabond souls... we who fall
> silent when we ought to be charming...
> ... we have Schubert for our brother.*

---

* Jacques Drillon (*Schubert et l'infini*).

Now those words were acquiring their full meaning.

Suddenly Jeanne, the young woman who had taken upon herself the task of ticket-selling, burst into the wings, her complexion pale and her face set. "Monsieur Peyre..." she said. "I have some bad news for you..."

"Constance Eisler? Is she..."

"The hospital called to let you know..."

A few meters away from me, Lenny was coming to the end of the Fantasy, playing with ever-mounting ardor and transport, not suspecting that he had been orphaned again...

The notes sounded, one at a time, thin, poignant, while the snowflakes were landing on the window, one by one, before melting into rivulets like tears on a cheek. The boy's hands barely moved on the keyboard—even his left hand, which had to search out the bass in the piano's lowest register, could do nothing to break the almost hieratic sensation of immobility—pain seemed to withdraw, and time to hold its breath. Was this because the end was imminent, or was it on the contrary a surge of life that bestowed a truly miraculous aspect on the piece as reborn under "the Wanderer's" fingers, making it purer, more crepuscular than ever before, suspended from the yellowed keys as though from a tight rope over the abyss?

A salvo of applause greeted the end of the recital's first piece. Moments later, Lenny was in the wings. He immediately asked, "How was it?"

I looked at him. His eyes were shining, his cheeks crimson, his face radiant. "Very good," I murmured, with an effort.

He turned a little gloomy. "You make such a face! What was not all right?"

"Lenny..."

I broke off. No, I couldn't do that—I had to let him finish his recital, at least...

"It was perfect," I said, starting over and hoping he'd chalk up my hesitation to admiration. "Go on, get out there! They're waiting for you..."

That theme, all sorrowful solitude, and tragic like the beloved song cycle—how had he not thought before of including it in his *Homage*, when after all his aim was to gather together the high points of the Schubertian oeuvre and meld them together into a single maddened, obsessive piece, in which from time to time Schubert's melodies would emerge, drawn up out of the chaos? Of the last three piano sonatas, Hermin had kept only the first movement of D. 960, mingling the B-flat major theme that opens the work with its development in C minor—an audacity of which he was, by the way, fairly proud; but how extraordinary, how could he have forgotten that poignant Andantino, the final song that was now becoming Lenny's "musical offering"? And while the melody was being repeated in octaves, Hermin felt his heart beat faster. All those works he'd been imagining as forming the framework of his *Homage*, did they not constitute, above all, "the Wanderer's" world—those march rhythms, those songs about rambling, that evocation, ultimately, of the pain of living? *Winterreise*...the Andante of the Opus 100 Trio...the Fantasia in F minor...the works Lenny most idolized, in short. And so Hermin yielded to the striking evidence: it wasn't an *Homage to Schubert* that he had undertaken to compose; no, it was an *Homage to the Wanderer*.

He went back onstage and immediately attacked the Brahms pieces. I've retained only a vague memory of this second part of Lenny's recital. Obviously, Constance's image was foremost in my mind, and I wasn't listening to the boy anymore. A single fact extracted me from my melancholy thoughts: at the end of the program, the captivated audience demanded an encore. We had agreed, should such a request be made, that the boy would play Liszt's variations on Schubert's Trauerwalzer*—*but to my great surprise, he launched into a work of my own composition, a short piece I wasn't even aware he knew how to play. It was a more than incongruous choice for an encore—the piece was far from a masterwork, and above all, it was atonal, that is, arid, the opposite of the short, brilliant pieces usually played in such circumstances but I realized that he was giving me a kind of present, and that in so ending his recital he meant to dedicate it to me. Had*

---

* "Mourning waltz."

he followed the plan and played the Trauerwalzer, *he would have unknowingly dedicated it to Constance.*

Now Hermin was listening, breathlessly, to the slow, sorrowful melody, played in octaves by the right hand, and at the same time dreading what was to come. The first theme was, technically speaking, easy to play—but the sudden surge, the acceleration, the crescendo, and then the central chaos, that tempest of sixty-fourth notes, the mighty breath that swept away everything in its path—how could the boy, in his weakened physical state, make all that audible? And so Hermin waited, breathing hard. Lenny was finishing the first part, attacking the garlands of sixteenths with his right hand, still playing softly, and then the left hand joined in, the tempo increased; but when would he break off, when would he fail?

After the recital, refreshments were waiting for the people who had participated in the realization of the project. As soon as Lenny returned to the wings, Devère, Guillemin, and about a dozen others monopolized him so completely that I could find no way to be, as I would have liked to be, alone with him. Besides, that excitement, at that moment, was convenient for my cowardice. Nevertheless, it was clear that Lenny had but one desire, namely to escape the admirers who were pressing around him and come over to me. He seized the first opportunity, and with a broad smile on his face, he asked, "So, you liked my encore?"

I said I had and quickly thanked him; then, without making a transition, I elected to give him the terrible news, aware that no circumlocution would be able to soften the blow I was about to deal him: "Lenny...your aunt is dead."

When he missed the first note, it was hardly more than a scratch, a tiny tear in the fabric of the music, but the E-flat that became an E-natural resounded endlessly in Hermin's ears, a focal point for all his anxieties. A few measures later, the boy's hands briefly moved away from the keyboard. He resumed, with a sort of distraught obstinacy, and penetrated the heart of the tempest. After a falling scale in thirty-second notes that covered the entire keyboard came some fortissimo chords in the right hand, moving from the lower register to the upper, chords that were all power and precision... Nonetheless, he played them without weakening, creating a sort of hallucinatory whirlwind that Hermin allowed to carry him away without resistance...

An abrupt outburst of coughing cleanly broke the boy's momentum. He lost control and then tried to regain it, but in vain. Bent double, unable to stop coughing, his features contorted into a rictus of pain, he was obliged to take his hands off the piano and place them on his chest, gasping, unable to go on. Hermin rushed to him, held out a hand to wipe away the tears streaming down his face, and murmured in a strangled voice, "It's going to be all right...Lenny, it'll be all right..."

"No…" the boy managed to articulate between gasps. "No…Hermin…Schubert…I cannot…"

The young composer didn't grasp the exact meaning of those words, but he felt despondency spreading through him: the music had been broken…"the Wanderer's" song was definitively over.

"Where does it hurt the most?" Hermin asked, drawing closer to the boy.

"Everywhere…I do not know…my chest…I feel like someone is sticking in a knife…"

Lenny collapsed.

For several seconds, he remained unmoving, as though dumbstruck, his eyes wide and staring. "Was?" he finally murmured.

"Your aunt…Deine Tante ist tot."

My resorting to German seemed to snap him out of his torpor. I saw his face fall apart. At the same moment, Devère came up behind him, unaware of the drama that was going on. "Leonard," he said, "you've certainly earned a drink. What can—"

"Verzeihen Sie mir!"* *the boy blurted out, jostling the gentleman aside and making for the exit.*

I gave Devère a stricken look and began to run after Lenny.

---

* "Excuse me!"

Stretched out on the sofa where Hermin had deposited him, Lenny was still breathing spasmodically, hoarsely, his eyes closed. In an attempt to assuage his friend's pain, Hermin started delicately massaging his chest, the movements recalling the night of the snowstorm, and suddenly images of that deranged moment, sensations he had striven to forget, came flooding into his mind. That evening, while he was trying to bring Lenny back to life, what exactly had he felt? Fear…fever…maybe desire—a desire that had dared to express itself in no other way than through that embrace, about which he had questioned himself the following day, but which had saved the boy more surely than any other gesture would have done…Yes, beyond the shadow of a doubt, that was the night when he had come closest to sharing Lenny's feelings, when he had nearly gone over to his side— *and that would have changed everything…*

I caught up with Lenny in the street and held on to his arm while he struggled to escape me.

"Lass mich in Ruhe…Lass mich in Ruhe…"* *he kept repeating, his voice strangled, his face disfigured by tears.*

"Lenny…" he murmured hoarsely. "Do you really think it's too late?"

The young man lowered his purplish eyelids for a moment. "Yes," he replied in a breath. "For me, it is too late."

---

* "Leave me alone…"

There was a period of silence. Then Hermin spoke again, without daring to look at him: "Thank you. For the piano."

"Do not thank me. The varied repeat is the best," replied the boy in a strangled voice.

Indeed... The return of the theme, transfigured by its passage through the cyclone—those little repeated notes in the upper register, echoing the melody, those subtle modifications, above all, that change of atmosphere—he hadn't been able to play that; he'd been prevented from doing so...

"No. What you did, it was..."

It was... what had it been, exactly? The music of a man who no longer belonged completely to this world, and who must have already glimpsed the absolute beauty of the hereafter—or so it seemed to Hermin, for whom the only proofs of God's existence were to be found in certain works, such as the *St. Matthew Passion* or the String Quintet in C.

"...It was beautiful."

"But interrupting Schubert is 'a crime against humanity,'" Lenny countered, with a poor excuse for a smile.

"In this case, I think he might forgive you."

There was a break in the conversation.

I put my arm under his shoulders, which were shaking with sobs. I thought he'd struggle even harder, but he did nothing... Or rather, he suddenly let himself collapse against me, burying his face against my throat and continuing to weep.

"Come on," I whispered. "Let's go home..."

He let me lead him all the way to the garret, leaning on me hard the whole time.

"And how about you? Do you forgive me?" Hermin didn't know what had compelled him to formulate that question, but now his whole being was waiting, yearning, for a reply, as if the uncertainty, without his realizing it, lay at the heart of his anguish.

The young man raised his head toward Hermin and stared at him for a few seconds with dull and weary eyes. "Yes," was all he murmured.

15

ERL-KING

Hermin stayed by the boy's side during the night. He'd expected him to thrash about, choke, maybe even rave deliriously. Instead he looked almost peaceful, even though he was gaunt from suffering, and he remained quiet, lying on the sofa near the fire. In the room's only light, provided by the flickering flames, Lenny's face took on the appearance of a wax mask, over which will-o'-the-wisps, "dominoes" in mauve cloaks trimmed with black wolf fur, passed in a phantasmagoria worthy of Couperin—but Hermin was instead thinking of that composer's sacred vocal work, the *Leçons de ténèbres,* while he gazed at the sleeper: *Passiontide,* he thought…For hours, like a sea captain watching over his doomed ship and clinging desperately to the helm, Hermin never took his eyes off Lenny's face, alert to the least shiver, the least murmur that would have announced a worsening of his condition. From time to time, he felt that Lenny, from under his half-closed, diaphanous eyelids, was watching him too.

After we got back home, Lenny said nothing. I understood only too well what he was feeling: that day, which he'd been anticipating for months and which he'd made into a celebration, had turned out to be one of the worst days of his life. He was alone again, bereft of the woman who had raised him. He hadn't even been able to assist her in her final moments…And while he was reveling in the spotlight, she'd been breathing her last.

Around dawn, the young man appeared to emerge from the torpor of the last several hours. Maybe some bird's "sunrise song" was what had awakened him, or maybe it was one of Hermin's movements. Half-illuminated by the pallid light coming through the window, Lenny sat up a little and spoke in a faltering voice, as though struck by a sudden thought: "Hermin…you remember…your postcard…*dio Abtei**…"

The young composer looked at him for a few seconds before realizing what he meant. Five years before, at the time of his move to Bourbonnais, Hermin had sent a picture postcard—something like throwing a bottle into the sea—to the music agency that promoted Lenny. Never having received a reply, he'd preferred to believe that the card

---

* "The abbey."

hadn't been passed on to the client. It pictured the abbey of Notre-Dame-des-Neiges, Our Lady of the Snows, located north of the Monts de la Madeleine...

"I remember."

"It's far from here?"

Hermin stared at the young man, shaken at having understood him all too well. "An hour, maybe. If there's not too much snow..."

"Well then, drive me there."

I looked at him helplessly. I'd never had any gift for consoling people—I could listen to them talk about their trouble, sure, but then, how to find the right words? And this particular case seemed to be precisely the sort about which there was nothing to say; no phrases would have the power to cushion the blow that had just struck him. But in spite of all that, I was required to say something...

The young composer had accepted, though with great reluctance, that the boy would prefer the Pommier Chenin to a hospital room; but to drive him somewhere else, on a whim—could he consent to such madness?

"You understand...I dream about that since...I wanted us to be there one time...It is beautiful, it is winter...Up there, maybe...I do not know...something will happen..."

Hermin clearly sensed that, underlying the boy's wish, there was a sort of obscure faith—perhaps religious in nature, perhaps not—but in any case a certitude, not easily shaken, concerning—what, exactly? His health? Their love? Most probably, he didn't know himself...

"You know, I don't think the abbey admits visitors."

"Hermin, do not say no...Please..."

I sat next to him on the sofa. He was curled up over his grief. "Lenny..." I began awkwardly. "You know I'm here to help you..."

He sniffled. "I know..."

And in fact, Hermin didn't refuse—truly, what could he refuse him at this point? He covered Lenny warmly, escorted him to the car, and then closed the door of the Pommier Chenin behind him.

He moved a little and snuggled up against me. "Put your arms around me...Please..."

I did so, clumsily.

They drove on slowly, against a background of snow-covered meadows. A few bare bushes and a few gray limbed trees swayed in the wind. An endless stream of thin snowflakes struck the car's windows. It was the irresolute hour that precedes the day: the sky, still a deep, nocturnal blue, was as though marbled with murky streaks, and in the distance dark clouds, the heralds of new storms, were gathering. The fantastic landscape spread out around them, and only a few deserted barns and a few farmhouses with smoking chimneys nestled in the little valleys, bearing witness to a human presence, however discreet, however forgotten by all.

Lenny appeared to be dozing. He'd closed his eyelids and slowly abandoned his head to the rhythms of the bumpy road. The rest of his body was immobile—except for his chest, which rose and fell with the raspy, almost cavernous sound of his breathing, which Hermin felt in his own body. Maybe out of fear of that respiration, like a death rattle, he pressed the radio button. He'd vaguely hoped to come upon a work that would deflect, if only for a brief time, the tragedy of the situation—some light music, by chance, or something amusing like *Pomp and Circumstance*, which they used to listen to and laugh?—but he froze, recognizing a lied by Schubert.

"Shall I turn this off?" he asked, holding his breath.

Lenny vaguely shook his head. "No...not Schubert... crime against humanity..."

Hermin smiled wanly and let the baritone's voice fill the interior of the car. *Nothing happens by chance*, he thought to himself.

"Hermin...," he whispered after a moment. *"I wanted to tell you..."* He stopped talking, short of breath.

"Yes?" I encouraged him.

"I...I was lucky to run into someone like you...Really... Without you, I would be lost..."

Of course, it occurred to him a little later, he should have expected something of the sort: at that early morning hour, there was always a program whose policy was to compare several interpretations of the same work. In this particular case, it was a selection of Schubert's lieder, each of them interpreted by a half-dozen different singers...Everything was fine as long as the song was "Frühlingstraum," the "Dream of Spring" from the *Winterreise* cycle—but his heart stopped beating when the next song began and he recognized the vehement triplets of "Erl-king."

The boy half opened his eyes. "'*Erlkönig...*'"

Without even noticing it, Hermin had accelerated. The sky, still violet, enveloped them in its stormy cape: "*Wer reitet so spät durch Nacht und Wind?*"*

"*I know I can't take your aunt's place, but you can count on me to help you!*"

"*Hermin...in any case, it is your help I need...*"

"*I know. She was aware of that. The last time we saw each other, she asked me to protect you...*"

His expression changed. "*You do this just because of her?*"

"*Of course not!*"

He relaxed a little.

The wind had picked up; the snow was lashing the car windows. Hermin briefly thought about taking the road to Renaison, as he should have done. The boy wouldn't notice anything...But then he immediately changed his mind. All he could accomplish by doing that would be a

---

* "Who's riding so late through night and wind?"

final betrayal. He might as well make him an offering of Notre-Dame-des-Neiges.

"*What I mean…*" *he began again, after a pause.* "*I am happy like this, really. With you in this garret…I feel like I am not going to know anything better…Except…*"

"*Except what?*"

"*Except…We cannot go on this way…*"

The first version was very expressive, almost expressionistic. So he dreaded all the more the imminent confrontation with the lied's final words, no, he couldn't, he'd cover his ears, not that, not the child's death, not that "*In seinen Armen, das Kind…*"

"*…war tot…*"* Lenny finished the line.

I looked at him without understanding. There was a slightly crazed gleam in his eyes.

"*What's the problem?*"

I had a confused feeling that we were no longer speaking about Constance, that now the subject was completely different, but I couldn't have said for sure when it had changed.

The radio had moved on to the second version of "Erl-king"—this one fiercer, also faster—when Lenny suddenly said, in a hushed voice, "*Ich sehe ihn…*"†

---

* "In his arms the child…was dead."

† "I see him…"

His eyes, with their dilated pupils, were fixed on a point beyond the window, as though magnetically drawn by something Hermin wasn't able to see.

"What?"

"*Der Erlkönig...Da...*"

"*Siehst, Vater, du den Erlkönig nicht...?*"* the radio continued.

The firs were twisting madly in the wind and splashes of snow spurting up from under Hermin's tires while the piano's hammering ostinato and the ascending crescendo of triplets in the left hand, more and more urgent, seemed to give the boy new vigor. He sat up in his seat, eyes wide-open, trembling slightly.

"Lenny, you're dreaming, it's the trees, the wind..."

"*In dürren blättern säuselt der Wind...*"†

"*Nein...*Hermin, I swear...over there..."

Hermin looked at him, panic-stricken. So that was it at last. Lenny was raving in delirium, swept away into Goethe's legend.

"Pay no attention, we're almost there..."

Lenny said nothing, but a glance at his anguished eyes suggested that the Erl-king was still pursuing him.

---

* "Don't you see, Father, the Erl-king there?"

† "Wind rustling dead leaves, that's what you hear..."

"You make...as if you do not see..."

"Don't see what?"

"We cannot keep going on...we cannot keep going on like this!"

Third version. A voice that rendered the song's three characters with incredible precision, especially the king—you could almost see the alders covered with gold, the beautiful girls dancing under them, and the train and the crown, infinitely multiplied in the mist...

"'Den Erlkönig mit Kron und Schweif?' / 'Mein Sohn, es ist ein Nebelstreif...'"*

"*Nebel...Leben und Nebel...*†️ My life will be lost in fog," the boy murmured, distraught.

"Calm down, please, calm down, it will be all right."

During the fourth version, Lenny turned his distraught face to him and murmured with the singer, "*'Ich liebe dich, mich reizt deine schöne Gestalt...'*"‡️ as he reached out a hand to touch Hermin's shoulder.

Hermin shuddered at the feeble contact and clenched his fists. Lenny was looking at him, desiring him, now and as always; he was at once the child and the Erl-king, and he, Hermin, was caught in the trap, once again.

---

* "'The Erl-king there, with train and crown?' / 'It is a patch of mist, my son.'"

† "Fog...Life and fog..."

‡ "'I love you, your beauty thrills my heart.'"

I couldn't very well see what he was getting at, but his despair gripped me. I tried to comfort him. "Lenny...I know it's hard...But you should remember that you've got your life ahead of you! You're going to be a concert pianist...you'll play my compositions...you'll find yourself a pretty girl, a musician..."

I had spoken those last words playfully, but the boy shot me a defeated look. "Shut up, Hermin," he said in a toneless voice.

At the height of his distress, Hermin was about to turn off the radio when he saw the sign for Notre-Dame-des-Neiges. "We're just about there...Hang on," he murmured.

Lenny vaguely nodded his head.

After a final bend in the road, the old nave rose up phantom-like among bare-branched trees. The road ended. Snowflakes were lashing the gray stones.

Hermin took Lenny in his arms, and the boy clung to him with all his meager strength. They had to halt several times on the icy path, both of them out of breath.

"*Wie schön...*" murmured Lenny as a timid ray of sunlight gave the stones of the bell tower a bluish cast. Then, almost immediately, he said, "Look...an almond in bloom..."

There was a tree whose every twig, covered with frost, did indeed seem to be budding   but the season of its flowering, of course, would not be coming anytime soon.

"It's not spring yet," Hermin whispered.

"Yes it is," the boy said.

I shut up. When I awakened the next morning, he had left.

He tightened his embrace. Hermin did the same. They were entwined in the snow, their faces almost touching—after a while, they unequivocally touched—the boy murmured something, looked at Hermin again—and as he slumped against him, Hermin thought he could still hear, resounding in his ears, the final words of "The Erl-king":

In seinen Armen das Kind war tot.

Thanks

to the entire team at Éditions Héloïse d'Ormesson for their investment in this adventure;

to Brigitte François-Sappey for her careful rereading;

to Philippe Marty for his contribution to the translation of the quoted texts;

to Bruno, my first reader;

and to my parents, for their support during these years of writing.

SARAH LÉON was born in 1995 and studied literature and musicology at the École normale supérieure in Paris. She won the 2012 Prix Clara for her novella, *Mon Alban*.

■

JOHN CULLEN is the translator of many books from Spanish, French, German, and Italian, including Philippe Claudel's *Brodeck*, Juli Zeh's *Decompression*, Chantal Thomas's *The Exchange of Princesses*, and Kamel Daoud's *The Meursault Investigation*. He lives in upstate New York.